A Night in a Moorish Harem

A Night in a Moorish Harem

Anonymous

MINT EDITIONS

A Night in a Moorish Harem was first published in 1896.

This edition published by Mint Editions 2021.

ISBN 9781513295626 | E-ISBN 9781513297125

Published by Mint Editions®

MINT
EDITIONS

minteditionbooks.com

Publishing Director: Jennifer Newens
Design & Production: Rachel Lopez Metzger
Project Manager: Micaela Clark
Typesetting: Westchester Publishing Services

Contents

Abdallah Pasha's Seraglio

H er British Majesty's Ship Antler, of which I was in command, lay becalmed one afternoon off the coast of Morocco. I did not allow the steam to be raised for I knew the evening breeze would soon make toward the land.

Retiring to my cabin I threw myself upon the sofa. I could not sleep for my thoughts kept wandering back to the beautiful women of London and the favours which some of them had granted me when last on shore.

Months had elapsed since then and months more would elapse before I could again hope to quench, in the lap of beauty, the hot desire which now coursed through my veins and distended my genitals.

To divert my mind from thoughts at present so imperative I resolved to take a bath. Beneath the stern windows which lighted my cabin lay a boat, into which I got by sliding down a rope which held it to the ship. Then I undressed and plunged into the cool waves. After bathing I redressed, and, reclining in the boat, fell asleep. When I awoke it was dark and I was floating along near the shore. The ship was miles away.

The rope which held the boat must have slipped when the breeze sprang up, and the people on the ship being busy getting underway had not noticed me. I had no oars and dared not use the sails for fear the Moorish vessels in sight would discover me. I drifted towards a large building which was the only one to be seen; it rose from the rocks near the water's edge. The approach to the place on which it stood seemed to be from the land side, and all the windows which I could see were high above the ground.

The keel of my boat soon grated on the sand and I hastened to pull it among the rocks for concealment, for it was quite possible I might be seized if discovered and sold into slavery. My plan was to wait for the land breeze just before dawn and escape to sea. At this moment I heard a whispered call from above. I looked up and saw two ladies looking down on me from the high windows above, and behind these two were gathered several others whom I could just see in the gloom.

"We have been watching you," said the lady, "and will try to assist you. Wait where you are."

She spoke in French, which is the common medium of communication among the different nations inhabiting the shores of the Mediterranean, and which had become familiar to me. I now thought this isolated building was a seraglio and I resolved to trust the ladies, who would run even more risk than myself in case of discovery.

After waiting some time, a rope of shawls was let down from the window and the same voice bid me climb. My discipline when a midshipman made this easy for me to do; I rose hand over hand and safely reached the window through which I was assisted by the ladies into the perfumed air of an elegant apartment richly furnished and elegantly lighted.

My first duty was to kiss the fair hands which had aided me, and then I explained the accident which had brought me among them and the plan I had formed for escape before dawn. I then gave my name and rank.

While doing this I had an opportunity to observe the ladies; there were nine of them and any one of them would have been remarked for her beauty. Each one of them differed from all the others in the style of her charms: some were large and some were small; some were slender and some plump, some blonde and some brunette, but all were bewitchingly beautiful. Each, too, was the most lovely type of a different nationality, for war and shipwrecks and piracy enable the Moorish Pashas to choose their darlings from under all the flags that float on the Mediterranean.

A lady whom they called Inez and whom, therefore, I took to be a Spaniard, answered me by bidding me in the name of all of them the warmest welcome.

"You are," she said, "in the seraglio of Abdallah, the Pasha of this district, who is not expected until tomorrow, and who will never be the wiser if his ladies seize so rare an opportunity to entertain a gentleman during his absence." She added, "We have no secrets or jealousy between ourselves," smiling very significantly.

"That is very unusual," said I. "How can any of you know whether he has any secrets with the one he happens to be alone with?"

"But one of us is never alone with him," said Inez. The blank look of consternation I had set them all laughing.

They were brimful of mischief and were evidently bent on making the most of the unexpected company of a young man. Inez put her hand on my sleeve. "How wet you are," said she. "It will not be hospitable to allow you to keep on such wet clothes."

My clothes were perfectly dry, but the winks and smiles that the young ladies exchanged as they began to disrobe me led me cheerfully to submit while they proceeded to divest me of every article of clothing.

When at length my shirt was suddenly jerked off they gave little affected screams and peeped through their fingers at my shaft; which by this time was of most towering dimensions. I had snatched a hearty kiss from one and all of them as they had gathered round to undress me.

Inez now handed me a scarf which she had taken from her own fair shoulders. "We can none of us bear to leave you," she said, "but you can only kiss one at a time; please throw this to the lady you prefer."

Good heavens! Then it was true, that all of these beautiful women had been accustomed to be present when one of them was embraced.

"Ladies," said I, "you are unfair. You have stripped me, but you keep those charms concealed which you offer to my preference. I am not sure now if you have any imperfections which you wish to keep covered."

The ladies looked at one another, blushed a little, then nodded and laughed, then began undressing. Velvet vests, skirts of lawn and silken trousers were rapidly flung to the floor. Lastly, as if at a given signal, every dainty chemise was stripped off and some of the most lovely forms that ever floated through a sculptor's dream stood naked before me. Was I not myself dreaming, or had I in truth been suddenly transported amid the houses of the seventh heaven?

For a while I stood entranced, gazing at the charming spectacle. "Ladies," said I at last, "it would be immodest in me to give preference when all are so ravishingly lovely. Please keep the scarf, fair Inez, and when I have paid a tribute to your fair charms, pass it yourself to another, till all have been gratified."

"Did he say all?" cried a little brunette.

"All indeed!" cried the rest in chorus, bursting into laughter.

"Every one," said I, "or I will perish in the attempt."

Inez was standing directly in front of me; she was about nineteen, and of that rarest type of Spanish beauty, partly derived from Flemish blood. Her eyes were sparkling brown, but her long hair was blonde. It was braided and coiled round the top of her head like a crown which added to her queenly appearance, for she was above the ordinary stature; her plump and well-rounded form harmonised with her height. Her complexion had the slight yellow tinge of rich cream, which was set off by the rosy nipples which tipped her full breasts and the still deeper rose of her lips and mouth.

She happened to be standing on one of the silken cushions which, singly and in piles, were scattered about the room in profusion. It made her height just equal to my own. As soon as I had made the speech last recorded, I advanced and folded her in my embrace.

Her soft arms were wound round me in response; and our lips met in a delicious and prolonged kiss, during which my shaft was imprisoned against her warm, smooth belly. Then she raised herself on tiptoe, which brought its crest amid the short, thick hair where the belly terminated. With one hand I guided my shaft to the entrance which welcomed it; with my other I held her plump buttocks toward me. Then she gradually settled on her feet again, and, as she did so, the entrance was slowly and delightfully effected in her moist, hot and swollen sheath. When she was finally on her feet again I could feel her throbbing womb resting on my shaft.

The other ladies had gathered round us; their kisses rained on my neck and shoulders, and the presence of their bosoms and bellies was against my back and sides—indeed they so completely sustained Inez and myself that I seemed about to mingle my being with them all at once. I had stirred the womb of Inez with but a few thrusts—when the rosy cheeks became a deeper dye, her eyes swam, her lips parted and I felt a delicious baptism of moisture on my shaft.

Then her head sank on my shoulder, the gathered sperm of months gushed from my crest so profusely that I seemed completely transferred with waves of rapture into the beautiful Spanish girl. Her sighs of pleasure were not only echoed by my own, but by those of all the ladies gathered around us in sympathy. They gently lowered us from this sustaining embrace to a pile of cushions. As they did so, with hardly any aid on our part, my diminished shaft was drawn out of Inez and, with it, some of my tributary sperm, which splashed on the floor.

"It was too bad of you, Inez, to take more than you can keep," said one of the others. She said it in such a pitiful tone it convulsed us all with laughter. As for me, I now realised the rashness of the promise I had made them all, but they gaily joined hands round Inez and myself and began a circling dance, their round, white limbs and plump bosoms floating in the lamplight as they moved in cadence to a Moorish love song, in which they all joined. With my cheeks pillowed against the full breasts of Inez, I watched the charming circle, which was like a scene in fairy land. Bracelets and anklets of heavy fettered gold glittered on their arms and legs; rings, necklaces and earrings of diamonds and rubies, which they had in profusion, glistened at every movement.

Each one had her hair elaborately dressed in the style peculiarly becoming to herself and there were no envious garments to conceal a single charm. I urged them to prolong the bewitching spectacle again and again, which they obligingly did. Then they gathered around me, reclining to rest on the cushions as near as they could get, in attitudes which were picturesque and voluptuous.

When we were thus resting I frequently exchanged a kiss or caress with my fair companions, which I took care to do impartially. Then it occurred to me that I would like to hear from the lips of each the most interesting and voluptuous passage from their lives. Again these interesting ladies, after a little urging, consented, and Inez commenced.

THE SPANISH LADY'S STORY

We lived in Seville. When I attained the age of sixteen my parents promised me in marriage to a wealthy gentleman, whom I had seen but twice and did not admire. My love was already given to Carlos, a handsome young officer who had just been promoted to a lieutenant for bravery. He was elegantly formed, his hair and eyes were as dark as night and he could dance to perfection. But it was for his gentle, winning smile that I loved him.

On the evening of the day that my parents had announced their determination to me, I had gone to be alone in the orange grove in the farthest part of our garden, there to sorrow over my hard fate. In the midst of my grief I heard the voice of Carlos calling me. Could it be he who had been banished from the house and whom I never expected to see again? He sprang down from the garden wall, folded me in his embrace and covered my hair with kisses for I had hidden my blushing face on my bosom. Then we talked of our sad lot.

Carlos was poor and it would be impossible to marry without the consent of my parents; we could only mingle our tears and regrets. He led me to a grassy bank concealed by the orange trees and rose bushes, then he drew me on his lap and kissed my lips and cheeks and eyes. I did not chide him, for it must be our last meeting, but I did not return his kisses with passion. I had never felt a wanton desire in my life, much less not when I was so sad. His passionate kisses were no longer confined to my face but were showered on my neck, and at length my dress was parted and revealed my little breasts to his ardent lips.

I felt startled and made an attempt to stop him in what considered an impropriety, but he did not stop there. I felt my skirts being raised with a mingled sensation of alarm and shame which caused me to try to prevent it, but it was impossible—I loved him too much to struggle against him and he was soon lying between my naked thighs.

"Inez," he said, "if you love me, be my wife for these few moments before we part."

I could not resist the appeal. I offered my lips to kisses without any feeling save innocent love, and lay passive while I felt him guide a stiff, warm object between my thighs. It entered where nothing had ever entered before and no sooner was it entered than he gave a fierce thrust which seemed to tear my vitals with a cruel pain.

ANONYMOUS

Then he gave deep sigh and sank heavily upon my bosom. I kissed him repeatedly, for I supposed it must have hurt him as much as it did me, little thinking that his pleasure had been as exquisite as my suffering had been. Just at that moment the harsh voice of my duenna resounded through the garden, calling, "Inez! Inez!" Exchanging with my seducer a lingering, hearty kiss, I extracted myself from his embrace and answered the call. My duenna eyed me sharply as I approached her.

"Why do you straddle your legs so far apart when you walk," said she, and when I came closer, "Why is the bosom of your dress so disordered and why are your cheeks so flushed?"

I made some excuse about climbing to get an orange and hurried past her to my room. I locked the door and prepared to go to bed that I might think uninterruptedly of Carlos, whom I now loved more than ever. When I took off my petticoat I found it all stained with blood. I folded it and treasured it beneath my pillow to dream upon, under the fond illusion that Carlos's blood was mingled there with my own.

For weeks afterwards I was so closely watched that I could not see Carlos. The evening preceding my marriage I went to vespers with my duenna. While we were kneeling in the cathedral a large woman, closely veiled, came and knelt close beside me. She attracted my attention by plucking my dress, and, as I turned, she momentarily lifted the corner of her mantle and I saw it was Carlos in disguise. I was now all alert and a small package was slipped into my hand. I had just time to secure it in my bosom when my duenna arose and we left the church.

As soon as I regained the privacy of my own room I tore open the package and found it contained a silken rope ladder and letter from Carlos requesting me to suspend it from the window that night after the family was at rest. The note was full of love. There was much more to tell, it said, if I would grant the interview by means of the ladder. Of course, I determined to see him. I was very ignorant of what most girls learn from each other, for I had no companion.

I supposed when a woman was embraced as I had been she necessarily got with child, and that such embraces therefore occurred at intervals of a year or so. I expected, consequently, nothing of the kind at the coming interview. I wanted to learn of Carlos if the child, which I supposed to be in my womb, would be born so soon as to betray our secret to my husband. When the family retired I went to my room and dressed myself elaborately, braiding my hair and putting on all of my jewellery. Then I fastened one end of the rope ladder to the bedpost and lowered the other end out of the window; it was at once strained by the ascending step of Carlos.

My eyes were soon feasted with the sight of my handsome lover, and we were soon locked in each other's arms. Again and again we alternately devoured each other with our eyes and pressed each other to our hearts. Words did not seem to be of any use; our kisses and caresses became more passionate, and for the first time in my life I felt a wanton emotion. The lips between my thighs became moistened and torrid with coursing blood; I could feel my cheeks burn under the ardent gaze of my lover; I could no longer meet his eyes—my own dropped in shame.

He began to undress me rapidly, his hand trembling with eagerness. Could it be that he wanted to pierce my loins so soon again, as he had done in the orange garden? An hour ago I would have dreaded it; now the thought caused a throb of welcome just where the pain had been sharpest. Stripped to my chemise, and even that unbuttoned by the eager hand of my lover, I darted from his arms and concealed my confusion beneath the bedcover. He soon undressed and followed me— then, bestowing one kiss on my neck and one on each of my naked breasts, he opened my thighs and parted the little curls between.

Again I felt the stiff, warm object entering. It entered slowly on account of the tightness, but every inch of its progress inward became more and more pleasant. When it was fully entered I was in a rapture of delight, yet something was wanting. I wrapped my arms around my lover and responded passionately to his kisses. I was almost tempted to respond to his thrusts by a wanton motion of my loins. My maidenhead was gone and the tender virgin wound completely healed, but I had still some remains of maiden shame. For a moment he lay still and then he gave me half a dozen deep thrusts, each succeeding one giving me more and more pleasure. It culminated at last in a thrill so exquisite that my frame seemed to melt. Nothing more was wanting. I gave a sigh of deep gratification and my arms fell nerveless to my sides, but I received with passionate pleasure two or three more thrusts which Carlos gave me, at each of which my sheath was penetrated by a copious gush which soothed and bathed its membranes.

For a long time we lay perfectly still; the stiff shaft which had completely filled me had diminished in size until it slipped completely out. Carlos at last relieved me of his weight by lying at my side, but our legs were still entwined. We had now time to converse. My lover explained to me all the sexual mysteries which remained for me to know, then we formed plans which would enable us after my marriage to meet often alone. These explanations and plans were mingled so freely with caresses that before my lover left me we had melted five times in each other's arms. I had barely strength to drag up the rope ladder after he departed. The day had now begun to dawn. I fell into a dreamless sleep and was awakened by my duenna pounding on the door and calling that it was nearly ten o'clock and that I was to be married at eleven. I was in no hurry but they got me to church in time. During the whole ceremony I felt my lover's sperm trickling down my thighs.

We all applauded Inez as she thus finished her story. While she was telling the story one of the ladies, whom I noticed to be the most fleshy of the number, cuddled up close to my side and suffered me to explore all her charms with my hand. During the description of the scene in the orange garden my fingers toyed with the curls between her thighs, and, as the story went on, parted the curls and felt of the lips beneath. She was turned partly on her belly against me so that this by-play was not observed. My fingers were encouraged by the lady's hand until two of them made an entrance and were completely enclosed in the hot, moist tissue. The little protuberance which all women have within the orifice, and which is the principal seat of sensation, was in her remarkably developed. It was as large as the end of my little finger. I played with it and squeezed it and plunged my fingers past it again and again; she manifested her pleasure by kissing me on the neck, where she had hidden her face.

When Inez described her first thrill in the bedroom scene my fingers were doing all in their power to complete the other lady's gratification, and this, too, with success, for they were suddenly bathed with moisture, and, at the same time, the lady drew a deep sigh, which was not noticed, for all supposed it to be in sympathy with Inez's story. Then she withdrew my hand and lay perfectly still. Inez was about to give her the scarf, but she lay so motionless that she handed it to another.

"This," said Inez, "is Helene, a Grecian lady. She will tell you a story and then she will do anything you wish."

My head was still pillowed on Inez's breast. Helene smiled, then stooped and kissed me. She was about medium height, very slender, but graceful and well rounded, and her skin was as white as alabaster. Her features were of the perfect antique mould and were lighted with fine grey eyes. Her glossy black hair was all brushed back to a knot just below the back of the neck, from which but a single curl escaped on either side and toyed with her firm but finely rounded bosom. The deep vermilion of her lips compensated for the faint colour of her cheeks, whose tinge was scarcely deeper than that of her finely cut ears. She was about twenty-two, and ripe to yield a charming embrace. I drew her down to a seat on my loins and begged her to begin her story.

THE GRECIAN LADY'S STORY

I entered the bridal bed a virgin. When the bridesmaids left me I trembled with apprehension and covered up my head under the bedclothes. It was because I had heard so many stories of the trials and hardships of a virgin on her marriage night and not because I had any antipathy towards my husband; On the contrary, I liked him. His courtship had been short, for he was a busy man in the diplomatic service of the Greek government. He was no longer young, but he was good-looking and manly, and I was proud that he had selected me from all the other Athenian girls. My heart beat still more violently when he entered.

He came to the side of the bed and, turning down the clothes from my head, he saw how I was agitated. He simply kissed my hand, and then went to the other side of the room to undress. This conduct somewhat reassured me. When he got into bed and took me in his arms my back was turned towards him. He took no liberties with any part of my person but began to converse with me about the incidents of the wedding. I was soon so calm that I suffered him to turn me with my face towards him, and he kissed me first on the forehead and then on the lips. After a while he begged me to return his kisses, saying that if I did not it would prove that I disliked him; thus encouraged I returned his kisses.

When I had so long lain in his arms that I began to feel at home, he turned me upon my back and unfastened the bosom of my chemise and kissed and fondled my breasts. This set my heart beating wildly again, but we kept exchanging kisses till he suddenly lifted the skirt of my chemise and lay between my thighs. Then I covered my face with my hands for shame, but he was so kind and gentle that I soon got so accustomed to the situation that I suffered him to remove my hands and fasten his mouth to mine in a passionate kiss. As he did so I felt something pushing between my thighs. It entered my curls there and touched the naked lips beneath. I felt my face grow hot with shame and lay perfectly passive. He must have been in bed with me two hours before he ventured so far. He had his reward, for a soft desire began to grow in my brain, the blood centred on my loins and I longed for the connection which was so imminent.

I returned him a kiss as passionate as he gave; it was the signal for which he had been waiting. I felt a pressure on the virgin membrane, not hard enough, however, to be painful. The pressure slackened and then pushed again and again. By this time I was wanton with desire and not only returned the passionate kisses, but I wound my arms around him. Then came the fateful thrust, tearing away the obstruction and reaching to the very depths of my loins. I gave a cry of mingled bliss and agony, which I could not help repeating at each of the three deep thrusts that followed. Then all was still and an effusion like balm filled my sheath in the place of the organ that had so disturbed it. A delightful languor stole over my frame and I went to sleep in my husband's arms.

In less than six months circumstances compelled me to deceive him.

After we had been married awhile our position required us to go a great deal in company. Card playing was very fashionable and the stakes got higher and higher. One night the luck ran terribly against me; I proposed for the party to double. My husband had gone on a journey a few days before and had left a large sum of money in my charge. It was nearly all his fortune. A portion of this money I now staked, thinking that the luck could not possibly go against me again, but it did. I was rendered desperate. Again I proposed to double—it would take all I had left if I lost. The ladies who were playing withdrew; the gentlemen were too polite to do so. The cards went against me. I felt myself turn dreadfully pale. The French ambassador, Count Henri, who was sitting beside me, was disposed to conceal my terrible embarrassment.

He was a handsome man, but, unlike my husband, he was very stalwart. His manners were very engaging. He kept up a stream of small talk till the others had dispersed to other parts of the room, then he offered to bring me on the morrow the amount I had lost. I turned as crimson as I had before been pale. I knew the price of such assistance. I made him no reply, my look dropped to the floor and I begged him to leave me, which he politely did. All next day I was nearly distracted; I hoped Count Henri would not come. My cheeks would burn as on the evening before and the blood all rush back to my heart. At three o'clock he came; the, valet showed him into the parlour, closed the door and retired. Count Henri must have known he was expected, for I was elegantly dressed in blue silk and my shoulders were set off with heavy lace.

I was so weak from agitation that I could not rise from the sofa to greet him.

"May I have the happiness," he said, "of being your confidant?" as he seated himself beside me, holding in one hand a well-filled purse and dropping the other around my waist.

I could not reject the purse. If I kept the purse I could not ask him to remove his arm. I was giddy with contending emotions.

"For God's sake, spare me," I murmured.

My head dropped, he caught it to his heart—I had fainted away. When I again became conscious I was lying on my back upon the sofa in the arms of the Count, the lace on my bosom was parted, my heavy skirts were all turned up from my naked thighs and he was in the very ecstasy of filling my sheath with sperm. It was this exquisite sensation which had restored me to consciousness, but I was too late to join in the ecstasy. His shaft became limber and small and I was left hopelessly in the lurch. Then I beseeched him to go as it was no time or place for this.

"Will you receive me in your bedroom tonight?" asked the Count, kissing my bare bosoms.

He had so excited my passions that I no longer hesitated.

"The front door will be unfastened all night," I replied, "and my room is directly over this."

Then he allowed me to rise.

I adjusted my disordered dress as quickly as possible, but I was not quick enough. The valet opened the door to bring in the card of a visitor. He saw enough to put me in his power. After the Count had gone I found the purse in my bosom; it contained more than I had lost, but my thoughts were not of money. My lips had tasted the forbidden fruit; I was no longer the same woman; my excitement had culminated in lascivious desire. I could hardly wait for night to come. When finally the house was still I unfastened the front door, retired to my room, undressed and was standing in my chemise with my nightgown in my hand ready to put on when the door of my room opened and Alex, the valet, stood before me with his finger on his lips.

He was a fine looking youth of seventeen, a Hungarian of a reduced family, who acted half in the capacity of secretary and half in that of valet for my husband. I could not help giving a faint scream, while I concealed my person as well as possible with the nightgown I held in my hands.

"My lady," said he, "I know all, but I shall be discreet. I only ask you to give me the sweetest proof of your confidence."

There was no help for it. With a murmured "For shame," I sprang into bed and hid under the bedclothes. He quickly undressed and followed me. My object was to dismiss him before the Count came;

I therefore suffered him to make rapid progress. He took me in his arms and kissed my lips and breasts and, as he raised my chemise, our naked thighs met. He was much more agitated than myself. I had been anticipating a paramour all the afternoon and he could not have known what reception would be accorded him. He could hardly guide his shaft to the lips that welcomed it.

As for myself, I began where I had left off with the Count. My sheath with wanton greediness devoured every inch that entered it and at the very first thrust I melted with an adulterous rapture never felt in my husband's embrace. Just at that moment I heard the front door softly open and shut. I pushed Alex away with force that drew his stiff shaft completely out of me.

"Gather up your clothes quickly and get into the closet," I said.

Madly eager as he must have been to finish, he hurried with his clothes into the closet as the Count entered. The Count came up and kissed me. I pretended to be asleep. He undressed hastily, and, getting into bed, took me in his arms. But I delayed his progress as much as possible. I made him tell me everything that had been said about my losses at cards. I used every artifice to keep him at bay until his efforts should arouse my passions. Then he mounted me and his stalwart shaft distended and penetrated me so much deeper than that of young Alex that it was more exquisite than before. Again the wild, adulterous thrill penetrated every part of my body. I fairly groaned with ecstasy. At that moment the front door loudly opened. It must be my husband unexpectedly returning.

"Good heavens, Count!" I cried, "under the bed with you."

He pulled his great stiff shaft out of me with a curse of disappointment that he could not finish and scrambled under the bed, dragging his clothes after him. My husband came in all beaming with delight that he had been able to return so soon. I received him with much demonstration.

"How it flushes your cheeks to see me," he said.

When he had undressed and come to bed I returned his caresses with so much ardour that he soon entered where Alex and the Count had so hastily withdrawn. I felt pleasant, but feigned much more rapture than I felt. To console the Count I dropped one of my hands down alongside the bed, which he was so polite as to kiss, and, as my husband's face was buried in my neck, while he was making rapid thrusts I kissed my other hand to Alex, who was peeping through the closet door. Then I gave a motion to my loins which sent my husband spending and repeated it till I had extracted from him the most copious gushes. It was too soon for me to melt with another thrill; my object was to fix him for a sound sleep, but the balmy sperm was so grateful to my hot sheath after the two fierce preceding encounters that I felt rewarded for my troubles. He soon fell sound asleep.

Then I motioned for the Count to go. With his clothes in one hand and his stiff shaft in the other he glided out. Soon after, we heard the front door shut and the disconsolate Alex cautiously came forth. With his clothes under his arm and both hands holding his rigid shaft, he too disappeared.

Here Helene finished. During her story I lay on my back with my head resting on Inez's bosom. Helene sat astride my loins with her face towards me, which gave me a fair view of her most secret charms. She somehow or other let me scarf fall over her thighs and beneath it her little tapering fingers began to play with my limber shaft. As the story proceeded it began to stiffen, and while she was describing the bedchamber scene she contrived to enter it into the crevice so directly above it. It rose and rose until it was almost rigid, vivified as it was by the close retreat in which it was hidden. She kept undulating her loins as the story went on till, just as she finished, I was nearly ready to spend. At the same moment I felt my shaft moistened with the moisture of the pretty Greek girl and she fell fainting in the arms of a lady close by.

The Moorish Lady's Story

L adies," she said, "you all know I am three months gone with child. You have now to learn what is equally true. I am a virgin still." "A virgin and with a child," they all echoed, several of them crossing themselves as they exclaimed. "Listen and you shall hear," proceeded Zuleika.

I was purchased from my parents in Fez, where we lived, by a young Moorish merchant. They, as well as myself, were delighted at the prospects which he promised of transferring me to the harem of some great Moorish pasha. The price paid was very high, as I was warranted a virgin. The next morning we joined the caravan for the coast; mounted on my camel I enjoyed the trip in the highest spirits. Ali, my master, rode beside me on a fine horse which he managed with grace and vigour.

His person was slender and his features, which were at the same time bold and amiable, captured my fancy. His attentions to my company were unremitting. His tent every night was pitched near my own to guard me from intrusion. The last night that we were on the road I had retired early and was just sinking to sleep as the darkness fell when Ali appeared in my tent.

"What is your will, my lord?" I asked. He bent down and kissed me. It was the first time he had done so.

"My wish is to make you my wife," he replied.

"And why should you not, my lord?" I asked.

Then he told me all his fortune was invested in my purchase and that it would only bring poverty and misery on us both. We mingled our regrets with caresses which grew more and more ardent, until I found myself lying beneath him with my bosom bared to his kisses and my naked thighs parted. Between them I felt a gentle pressure which penetrated the hair and touched the more sensitive lips beneath. I hoped that Ali had determined to marry me. I knew he would if he despoiled me of my virginity, for then my great market value would be gone.

I lay passive with my eyes shut. A soft desire ran through my frame centring at the lips where Ali was pressing and making the pressure delightful. The longer he continued in this position the more I wished for a deeper and more satisfying thrust. But the gentle pushes he gave barely parted the outside lips. I could feel that they were stopped by the virgin membrane that barred any further entrance. I grew wild with desire—I strained him to my bosom, and, pressing my mouth to his, I was relieved of a melting thrill.

At the same moment I felt Ali's answering throb and a gush of his sperm penetrated to the depths of my loins, far within the still unbroken curtain of my virginity. For a long time after we lay in a voluptuous but motionless repose. Then Ali tore himself from my arms.

"I must go," he said, "for I cannot resist another such temptation."

ANONYMOUS

"It is three months since that sweet but imperfect connection, which it is now certain will result in my being a mother."

"And has no man touched you since?" I asked with deepest interest, as I took the splendid Moorish girl blushing in my lap.

"I can tell you," replied Inez, "why the Pasha, who never before suffered a woman to remain a virgin a single night in his harem, has spared her."

He purchased her from Ali the day the caravan reached its destination. After having her examined by the old woman in his employ, she was brought here, and the same evening as soon as he had finished his supper he threw his handkerchief to her. She retired to receive him in her room alone, as only a virgin in this harem has the privilege of doing, for, as you already know, it is customary for us to receive the Pasha's embraces when we are all present. I noticed Zuleika looked very reluctant—she was doubtless thinking of Ali, from whom she had so recently parted. I overtook her at the door of the bridal chamber.

"Let me take your place for tonight," said I. "We are the same size, and complexions will not show in the dark. The Pasha shall never know."

"Can you indeed manage it?" she asked. "If so, you are welcome."

Then she hurried away and I entered the bridal chamber in her place, undressed, extinguished the light and got into bed. Before a great while the Pasha came. He kissed me on the back of the neck, for I buried my face in the pillow like a bashful girl. Then he hurriedly undressed, and, stretching himself beside me, took me in his arms. My heart was beating violently for the success of my bold scheme, but this agitation he took for virgin fright.

I answered in whispered monosyllables to his questions and shrank from every caress he bestowed on my bosom and thighs. He became, as I intended he should, only the more eager. When at length he mounted me, I covered my face with both hands as if in a paroxysm of shame, and wrapping one of my legs over the other, held them tightly together. He had to lie with his thighs parted over mine. In this position he guided his crest between them, which worked its way between the hair and began to enter the tightly squeezed lips beneath. My passions had become so thoroughly aroused by this time that I could scarcely help opening my thighs and letting him have free entrance. My monthly period was just passing off, in the latter part of which a woman is peculiarly susceptible to desire, but I made him gain his way by the hardest pushing. Not only were my thighs locked, but I tightly contracted the muscles of my sheath at the lips.

He would give a fierce but ineffective thrust, then he would squeeze and suck my breasts, until at last my wantonness became uncontrollable and I gave way with a feeling that unnerved me, letting his shaft plunge into the hilt. He spent profusely with a long sigh of triumphant satisfaction. I gave a sigh equally profound; I could not help it. But it only completed his delusion, for he thought it was caused by pain I suffered at the rupture of my maidenhead.

He petted and consoled me with kisses and caresses till we were both ready for another embrace. This time he did not expect me to be especially coy at his embrace. Then he fell asleep. I knew he would awake in the morning with a stiff shaft, so just before dawn I went and took a bath and put on my most seductive apparel, adorned myself with all my jewellery and perfumed myself with musk.

Soon I heard him call, "Zuleika, Zuleika!" I hastened to his bedside.

"Zuleika begs that you will excuse her my lord," said I. "Pray have some mercy on the poor girl."

Then I turned down the sheet and exposed the blood stains occasioned by my monthly period.

"See," said I, "you have butchered her."

"Then you must come to bed with me," said he. This was just what I sought and I lost no time in doing so and for the third time I got all I wanted.

I nez ended amid the hearty laughter of the ladies. As for me, I had been caressing Zuleika; her plump bosom, her smooth belly and her grand thighs passed in review under my hand. She concealed her face on my bosom but she made no resistance.

Perhaps she no longer thought of Ali. I ventured even to insert my forefinger between the lips which concealed her maidenhead. It stretched from side to side of her entire sheath, save the little orifice that is never closed.

She raised her face, which was overspread with crimson blush; her eyes were shut, but her mouth pouted for the kiss which my lips fastened upon it. The voluptuous stories and the wanton situation had done their work upon her. My intrusive finger perceived the throbbing of the lips between which it was inserted. My shaft had become as rigid as bone. The glands clung to the base all ready for action. As soon as Inez finished speaking I laid Zuleika on her back upon the cushions, spread her thighs wide open and mounted her. My crest was at once buried where my finger had lately explored. I gave a push that strained the virgin membrane, but it had the strength which characterised the rest of her splendid physique, and bounded back like India rubber.

Her whole form quivered at the touch. Furious with lust I wrapped my arms around the small of her back and braced my whole strength for another thrust. My crest went plunging in, tore through the curtain of her virginity and rammed against her pregnant womb. "Allah! Allah!" she cried, tossing her arms wildly upwards and rolling her eyes towards heaven. Whether her pain or her pleasure was most exquisite I did not know, but my whole being seemed to centre in my loins and gush into the superb Moor. Then I sank prostrate and exhausted on her bosom with everything gratified.

"The baby has been fed," said Inez, which caused another laugh among the ladies.

"See Zuleika," said another in an alarmed tone, "she has fainted."

Zuleika had indeed become very pale. One gave her a glass of water and bathed her forehead; another took the scarf from her hand and staunched the blood which was flowing from between her thighs. I supported her head on my arm and gave her kisses which before long she began to return. Then she threw one of her thighs over me to conceal the trace of her wound, saying to the lady who had been using the scarf that she bequeathed it to her. This lady's name was Laura, and she was an Italian. It was the same who had melted at the touch of my fingers during the first story.

She was about twenty-four and the most fleshy lady in the room. Her immense bosom and buttocks quivered as she moved, but rounded out again in perfect contour when she was still. She had dimples on her cheeks and chin, dimples at her elbows and knees and dimples at her hips. Her features were very pleasing, with a rosy mouth, a saucy retrousse nose and eyes that were dark in expression and shaded by long lashes. She wore her long hair in puffs supported by a tall shell comb—perhaps to add to her height, which was only medium, notwithstanding her enormous weight. Still her waist was not overgrown, and her wrists and ankles were pretty. "I think I shall have time to tell a long story," she said, glancing ruefully at the diminished little object between my legs. Amid the titters caused by this remark, she seated herself on the opposite side of me from Zuleika, where she could caress my genitals with one of her hands while she proceeded with her story.

The Italian Lady's Story

I am sorry to confess that I did not possess a maidenhead when I was married. It caused a jealousy and suspicion in my husband's mind which I could not eradicate. When I was a girl of sixteen at school in a convent, one of my companions handed me an improper book. It contained the amours of the ancient gods and goddesses. They were painted so minutely that it left nothing to be imagined, and it so fascinated me that I at once began it. I retired to my room and bolted my door to devour it undisturbed. I took off my clothes, and, putting on my dressing gown, lay on my bed to read at my ease. Alone as I was, my cheeks burned at the lascivious descriptions in the book. Then I longed to be in the place of one of the goddesses or nymphs in the wanton adventures. The blood coursed hotly through my veins. I felt the need of something which I never had before, something to quench the seething heat for the first time generated in my loins. I put my hand on the seat of desire; the young hair which grew there had not yet become thick enough to protect the lips beneath from the most casual touch.

They grew sensitive under my hands, and, after I read of the rape or seduction of one goddess after another, my fingers slipped in between the lips and, by a gentle movement, afforded me some pleasure. The motion to be satisfactory had constantly to be increased until I came to the raptures of Venus in the arms of Mars. My wantonness became uncontrollable, a sensation such as was described in the book partially thrilled me, I plunged my fingers in the whole length to complete it and away went my maidenhead. It hurt me cruelly, but I did not care for that. I knew the irreparable injury which my folly had caused. I was disgusted with my folly and flung the book away. I never put my fingers on that same place again, much less let any man touch me.

One night I told my husband all the pitiful truth, but he was still suspicious. We lived in Naples. He was a professor in the university. He seemed to think of nothing but science. For two or three weeks together he would go to bed with me and rise again without even having put his hand under my chemise, and still more rarely gave me the marital embrace. But I did not suffer myself to care for that. One day I accompanied him on a journey to another town to look for some rare manuscripts of which he had heard. We were going on a lonely road through a forest when a large and gaily dressed brigand stepped from the woods and stopped the horse.

"Resist at your peril," he said, pointing a cocked pistol and leading the horse and vehicle into a lonely side path.

When we had got some distance from the main road he stopped and ordered us to get out. He fastened the horse to a tree and then procured some cord from his pocket with which he firmly bound my husband's hands behind his back; then, having also tied his feet together, he bound him to a tree and searched him for valuables.

"Now, my fair lady," said he, approaching me, "it is your turn."

"Take my jewellery—it is all I've got—and let me go."

"Thank you for the present," he said, "but you have got something else I prize still more."

Then he put his arm around my waist and attempted to kiss me. I struggled to get free, while my husband alternately cursed and entreated him, but all to no purpose. I tried to get close to my husband, but it only served to make him a nearer witness of what followed. I was suddenly tripped and thrown on the grass with the brigand on top of me. He held both of my hands on the ground above my head with one of his own; with the other he tore open the front of my dress and explored my bosoms, which he rifled with his hand and sucked with his mouth. Then he pulled up the skirts of my dress and petticoat. I redoubled my exertions and even got one of my hands loose; but by this time he had forced open my thighs with his knee and lay between them.

He pinioned both of my hands as before, leaving one of his hands free to get out his shaft and enter it into me. Then every struggle I made seemed to work him in further. I could only sob with rage and shame. The brigand, with his Herculean strength, did his will with me right before my husband's eyes, who had by this time howled himself hoarse with curses. Angry and mortified, as I was, it began to feel good. To escape this crowning humiliation I made one tremendous effort to get free. I was pinioned to the ground by a fierce thrust of my ravisher, and then I felt the cream of his strength entering my loins. The sensation almost thrilled me, but his powerful grasp so relaxed that by a great effort I extracted myself from beneath him. I ran to my husband and began untying him, but the brigand seized me by the wrists and dragged me some distance up the pathway.

Then he suddenly thrust his hand into my bosom and gave it a parting squeeze, kissed my averted face and let me go. I ran back trembling and sobbing to my husband, whom I unbound as rapidly as possible. He unfastened the horse without saying a word or even helping me into the vehicle and drove home in silent and sullen gloom. It was too cruel. I had been able to endure his suspicions with regard to the loss of my maidenhead, because it had been the result of my own folly. But this dreadful rape had been committed without any fault of mine.

He never afterward lay with me or held me in his embrace, although we continued to live together. A young woman in the bloom of vigour and just well enough initiated with the mysteries of matrimony, I was condemned to celibacy. Wanton thoughts occupied my mind until my sheath would throb and its lips moisten and swell with desire for hours together. I reverted to the means that had despoiled me of my maidenhead, but I was in a state of constant agitation. My husband suspected me; I determined to give him a cause. It seemed as if no one man could satisfy me now; I longed for an opportunity to give rein to my passions.

At this time a Russian fleet came into the harbour. My sister's husband was a naval officer in the harbour and it devolved on him to help entertain the Russian officers. So my sister gave a masked ball to which they were invited. My husband would not go but he made no objections to my attending and staying all night at my sister's house. My room opened from the passage that connected the ballroom with the conservatory. I procured a long and ample nun's robe which covered me from my throat to my toes; it had also a cowl which concealed my head and face. Under this disguise I had the dress—or rather the undress—of a dancing girl; a vest of cloth of gold and a skirt of the thinnest lawn were absolutely the only articles of which it consisted, besides my stockings and slippers. The vest had no sleeves or shoulders and exposed my bosom clear to the nipples. If I moved quickly the short and gauzy skirt showed my naked thighs. As soon as the guests began to mingle on the floor I touched the arm of a stalwart Russian officer; he, like all the other guests, was masked, but I knew he was a Russian by his fair hair.

"Follow me," I whispered.

We entered the passageway described, and finding it clear I led him to my room.

"What a dainty bower!" he said in French. "Will its sweet-voiced occupant be pleased that we both unmask?"

He removed his mask and disclosed one of those ruddy countenances with bright eyes and fair hair which always so bewitch an Italian lady. I flung back my nun's disguise and stood revealed to him in the costume of a lascivious young dancing girl. The young Russian seemed to admire my dark Italian complexion as much as I admired his northern hue. He knelt and kissed my hand.

"Can you pity a bride," said I, "whose husband neglects her?"

A flush of pleasure crossed the officer's face which made my looks seek the floor.

"It would be the supremest happiness," he said, "to pity and console you."

He clasped his arms around me and our lips met. The moment I had so long desired for had now come. I was borne in his strong arms to the bed, where I lay palpitating with desire while he stripped off his outer garments. Then the fervour of our kisses and caresses showed the length of time we had both suffered without an embrace. My dress formed no obstacle to his caresses, either to my bosom, which he fairly seemed to devour, or to my thighs, which he squeezed and patted. I guided his shaft with one hand while with the other I parted the hair encircling the lips to receive it. How stiff it was, and yet how full of life and warmth! How tight, and yet how soft and lubricated was the place it was entering! I was so eager I had not even affected to be coy.

"How delicious!" he exclaimed.

"How exquisite!" I replied.

He gave a thrust which enabled me to take his shaft in to the hilt. Then he gave another and another, each successive one more greedily swallowed. Flesh and blood could no longer endure the rapture that was concentrated at my very loins! I thrilled from my womb to my very fingertips! I melted and bathed his hot crest; his responsive gush drenched my glowing womb. It seemed as if we were being fused together at the point of contact. Then our muscles relaxed closely in the moisture and we engaged for awhile in voluptuous repose.

"Now kiss me and go," said I, "and if you value the favour I have granted you, leave this house at once."

My object was to fill his place with another handsome Russian, who might come fresh to the encounter, and whose genitals my wanton hands might explore and my wanton desire ravish. Months of longing were to be supplied by one night of boundless lust. Six times more before the ball broke up I took a Russian officer to my room and dismissed him as before—and each time a different one. Each time

I was completely melted, and my Italian moisture mingled with the Russian sperm. The next morning my glass showed me that I had dark and sunken circles around my eyes, and I was somewhat languid, but for a few days at least I was not troubled with desire.

The fat and charming Italian lady had been gently fondling my genitals all the while she had been speaking and my shaft had begun to rise at the delicate attention. When she finished her story she knelt before me with her forehead on the carpet, laughingly saying, "Salaam, alirkoum," which was the Moorish to signify she was at my service. Her large, round buttocks were elevated in the air and looked so temptingly smooth and soft that I mounted her in that position as a stallion would mount a mare. She seemed nothing loth and my halfstiffened shaft worked its way in past the swollen lips— past the extraordinary protuberance within, which my fingers had first discovered—and buried itself amid the moist and clinging folds of her sheath. My loins sank into her fat buttocks, which yielded as I pushed, till my stones were hidden in her hair like eggs in a nest. Still I kept pushing into the yielding mass without once drawing back till my shaft grew stiff with the delightful sensation, and my crest exchanged a wanton desire with her womb. I held her firmly by clasping a great, soft breast in either hand. A few minutes more and I would have paid tribute to her voluptuous loins, but Laura could not wait.

With a sigh of satisfaction her frame became limp, her knees gave way and she sank flat upon her belly. My shaft drew out of her far more stiff than it went in. The same accompanying sucking noise that ended my connection with Helene set them all to laughing.

"I must take a measurement," said one of them and, taking off her bracelet, she clasped it around my shaft.

But the clasp would not fasten. The bracelet was not large enough. Then they all tried their bracelets on with the same result.

"How shall we measure its length?" said one of them.

"Four of you have that measure already," said I, "and you know I promised it to all of you. Please let me take some measurements now," I added, unwinding the garter from the leg of the nearest lady. It was a piece of strong tape and suited my purpose admirably.

I measured the size of all their bosoms and the circumference of their thighs, and then, amid laughing protestations, I parted the hair between each pair of thighs and measured the length of their slits. In the last measurement they all seemed to be desirous of being the smallest, as in the other they each wished to be the largest in size. The young Persian who told her story later in the evening bore off the palm in the last contest. Her diminutive slit looked all the more cunning that the hair around it was hardly long enough to curl. Zuleika had the largest bosoms, while the thighs of Laura defied competition.

"Here, Anna, take the scarf," interrupted the Italian, "and tell the Captain something about Circassia."

The lady thus addressed was about nineteen years of age and she was very tall and slender. Her limbs were finely tapered; so was her round waist, which I could have spanned with my two hands. Her nicely cut breasts were as erect as if they had been carved from alabaster, which her skin resembled in whiteness. The hair on her small head was of the palest blonde, but that at her loins was fiery red, which I had read was a sign of uncontrollable wantonness. If so, this lady's face gave no indication of it.

Her large blue eyes looked at you with the innocence of childhood, and the delicate roseate hue of her cheeks varied at every changing emotion. She did not seem sensible, however, of the privilege conferred upon her by the scarf. She stretched herself between my thighs, where she leaned with her elbow on the cushion, supporting her graceful head with her hand. Her bosom rested on my loins and my shaft was imprisoned by her snowy breasts from between which its red crest peeped out while she looked me in the face and told her lascivious story.

THE CIRCASSIAN LADY'S STORY

The powerful old chief to whom my mother was married had no children of his own. I was her only child by a former marriage and her fondness was all centred on me. Our religion, which was the Greek, forbade a plurality of wives. The old chief was not likely to have a direct heir, and, as he was now seventy, her great object was to have him confer on me the succession to the principality; this last he consented to do if she would countenance his amours with other women. She consented to do so and the strange compact was formed—I was present as witness. Unknown to either of them, I had been in the habit, for a long time, of frequenting a little alcove in their bedroom where a few books were kept. It was separated by a curtain from the rest of the room and communicated also with my chamber by a sliding panel. This secret panel, which I had accidentally discovered, was a kind often met with in such old castles as we inhabited. It was known to me alone, or, if the old chief knew it was there, he never thought of it. I had there witnessed all the secrets of the marriage chamber, and of course my passions were rapidly developed.

My mother was still plump and handsome; she enjoyed keenly the marriage embrace, but always had to work very hard in order to finish the tardy rapture of the old chief. On the occasion of the compact I heard her tell him she could give him all he wanted. He could only reply that a man liked a variety.

"Very well," said she, "make out the deed for Anna's succession and I will not only countenance but assist in your amours. We can in that way at least secure secrecy and avoid scandal, for no one will suspect a wife of conniving at her husband's amours."

The old chief then confided to her that the present object of his desire was Leuline, the handsome wife of the steward of the castle. The next evening I was at my post early. My mother had already managed with Leuline. She was a large and voluptuous-looking woman with dark hair and blue eyes; her bosoms were not much developed, but her thighs were immense. She got into bed with my mother and pretended to be asleep when the old chief came in. He undressed and got into bed with them and mounted Leuline, who lay with her head on my mother's arm, close to her bosom. An expression of pleasure stole over Leuline's face, which became more ineffable at every thrust. At last their mingled sighs and the stillness that followed gave proof that the embrace had been mutually satisfactory.

"You can imagine," said Anna, smiling at the other girls, "how I longed for the embrace of a man."

Plans for future meetings and jokes at the expense of Leuline's husband filled up the time, together with explorations of Leuline's charms, till the shaft of the old chief grew again stiff. He plunged it into Leuline's great loins, and she enjoyed it so highly that she finished and left him in the lurch. I could hardly restrain myself, I so longed for the thrusts that were now wasted on Leuline. My mother must have felt the same way, for she asked the old chief to let her finish him. He had more than once sucked her fine bosoms during this onset.

He now transferred his crimson crest dripping with Leuline's moisture. The energy with which my mother received him made me fairly wriggle my loins in sympathy. She wound her arms around him and raised up her loins to meet his descending thrusts, then their frames were convulsed for a few moments with the culminant rapture and they subsided into perfect repose. I had often before felt wanton emotion at my post of observation; I now left the alcove in a frenzy of lust. I wanted a man, and that immediately; I was about to seek one of the sentinels at his post, to confer my virginity on the first rude soldier I met on the cover of the ramparts, when I remembered Tessidor, a young priest, who was attached to the chapel of the castle. He was a delicate-looking youth of about seventeen, with a countenance which indicated the purity of his character.

I went to his room and timidly knocked on the door. To my timid knock the answer was delayed; when at last he said "come in", I saw that he had employed the interval by slipping on a nightshirt, for he had been just about to retire.

He looked astonished, as well he might, when he saw me. "I have come to make a confession and ask your counsel," said I.

"Had we better not go to the chapel?" he asked. "It is better here,"

I said, "for the subject is a worldly one, though of much importance to me. I love a young man who is indifferent to my preference, nay, he is even insensible to my love. I would have my parents hint to him that his addresses would be accepted; but I am meant to marry a soldier and he is not a soldier. What shall I do?"

"Strive to forget him, my lady," was the reply.

I stood a moment with my look cast on the ground and my cheeks burning.

"Cruel man," I said, "it is you who have my heart."

My head dropped forward, I seemed about to fall, but I put up my mouth for the kiss which he bent over to impress upon it. Regrets were then mingled with kisses, while I allowed my wrapper to fall open and expose my bosoms. He ventured timidly to kiss them; his kisses became more and more ardent. I had got him at last where a man has no conscience. He stretched himself on the bed beside me, took me in his arms: our lips were glued together. As much by my contrivance as his own, but he did not know it, my wrapper and dressing gown opened, and a skirt and chemise were all that separated a stiff little object from my thighs. Fired by lust as I was, I had shame enough left to leave the removal of these slight obstructions to him. I could hardly wait upon his timidity.

I must have been the first woman he had ever entered, for he was very awkward in guiding his crest to the lips that yearned to close upon it. It was a little thing, but very stiff. At last it penetrated me a little way and I felt the touch of his crest against my maidenhead like an electric shock; it set all my nerves tingling with pleasure, and expectant of the coming connection, I could no longer even feign modesty. I involuntarily wrapped my arms around him and he gave the fateful thrust. His little crest pierced through my maidenhead with a cutting pain which I felt no more than a bulling heifer would have felt the stroke of a switch. The pain was drowned in overwhelming pleasure. The thrill swept over every fibre in my frame, not only at the first thrust, but three times successively, and at each plunge I gave a sigh of rapture.

Then my tense muscles relaxed and I received with pleasure at least a dozen more thrusts. Something was still wanting. It was the gush of sperm that Tessidor at last poured into my heated sheath like balm. He sank heavily upon me for a few minutes with his face buried in my neck. I was enjoying a voluptuous languor, when I felt his little shrunken crest floating out of my sheath with the mingled blood and sperm. Remorse had already seized him. He raised himself on his elbow and gazed pitifully into my face. I was past blushing so I covered my face with my hands.

"I have ruined you," he said, "wretch that I am, heaven forgive me!"

He got up from the bed without even giving me another kiss and knelt before his crucifix.

"Will you join me in asking heaven for mercy on my sin?" he beseeched.

I made some excuse and fled from the room. The next morning I heard that he had gone to join a convent in the mountains. By this time I had come to the conclusion that I had let him off too quickly. I had not had enough. Perhaps a warm bath would help to soothe me. There was a large bath half the size of a room and deep enough when full to cover my breasts; there was a door to it from my room and one from my mother's; she was busy at this time in the morning with her servants. It was the old chiefs time to take a bath and he always had the warm water; I determined to share it with him. I had heretofore doubted whether the old chief would want to touch his wife's daughter, but my success with the young priest gave me courage.

I took off all my clothes in my room and peeped through the door. He was floating on his back playing with his shaft, which dangled limber in the water. I had most always seen it stiff, and I promised myself the pleasure of getting it in that position, which I preferred. Pretty soon he came to the side towards me, where he could not be seen by me; now was the time for me to come in as if I had not known he was there. I opened my door suddenly and ran and jumped into the water. I swam across the bath, turned around and became the picture of astonishment at seeing him. I first covered my face with my hands, then covered by bosom with one hand and my loins with the other. I did not scream; that might bring my mother. Then I turned my back on him. The side of the bath where I stood was perpendicular. He stood by the sloping side where we got out—of course I had to stay.

"It's all right, Anna," he said, "we will have a nice bath together."

I started to dodge past him, but of course he caught me. "I shall scream," said I, but of course I did not scream.

I was fast in his arms, his stiffening shaft crushing against my buttocks and each of his hands squeezing one of my bosoms. My apprehensions of reluctance on his part were all departed, so I kept up more show of resistance. I struggled to get away, but only struggled harder to get around in front of him. This brought my back to the sloping side of the bathtub, against which he pressed me. Half standing and half lying my head was still above water. The wantonness of the situation and the warmth of the water made the bath seem like a voluptuous sea.

Of course I had put both arms around him to keep from sinking; his hands were thus both at liberty. He needed them both to work his half-stiffened shaft into me. Leuline and my mother only the night before had taken the starch out of it; nothing but the excitement of such a kind of rape would have stiffened it at all. Half limber as it was, it completely filled me, paining me a little at first, but gradually feeling better and better, pervading all through me with the most lascivious sensation. The warm water churned in and out of my sheath at every thrust with a feeling like gushing sperm. All the water in the bath seemed to be of the male gender, and all of it embracing me and administering to my lust.

For fully five minutes I abandoned myself to the delicious dissolving feeling, not as thrilling as the young priest had caused the night before, but more prolonged. Even after it had subsided and died away, the plunges of the old chief were still pleasant. Finally his shaft became for a moment rigid deep within me, he gave a throb or two which deprived him of his strength and he no longer supported me. I scrambled from his arms up the side of the bath and, regaining my own room, shut the door and sank exhausted on the bed. We never pursued the intrigue, as the terror of my mother was too much before our eyes. Besides I was a few days after engaged in an amour with Rudolf, the handsome young captain of the guard, while the old chief had been supplied with a fresh bedfellow by my mother.

This time, in the place of Leuline, it was a young maid, who timidly blushed—for I still amused myself occasionally peeping through the alcove. A short time afterward the old chief was slain in battle and the sagacity of my mother was rewarded, for I succeeded peaceably to the principality. But my mother swayed the real power. I was willing she should do so, provided she did not interfere with my amours. It was by her advice that I did not marry.

"A virgin chieftain will be popular with the people, and you can control men," she would say, "far better unmarried."

In fact, Rudolf, captain of the guard, was my abject slave, and so were Cassim and Selim, two of the bravest young chiefs in the army. I admitted them all to my bed in turn, Rudolf the most frequently, for he was powerfully built and had genitals correspondingly large. When I wished to be tickled deeply, the tall and slender Selim received the secret summons to my chamber. Cassim was short and stout—it was agreeable sometimes to be stretched without being deeply penetrated. Each of these suspected that the others also enjoyed my favour, but they were not certain of it.

One evening I invited them all to my secret apartments. The sideboard had been replenished, the servants had been dismissed for the evening and the doors locked. I was dressed in a purple velvet bodice with a petticoat of red silk. I had on my richest lace and jewellery and the crown of the principality was on my brow. The handsome young officers glittered in their splendid uniforms; suspense and curiosity were mingled in their countenances. I waited until several toasts had been drunk in my honour while my wanton eyes devoured the fine proportions of the young men, then I thus addressed them:

"Should not a Circassian princess have as many privileges as a Turkish pasha?"

"Certainly," they all replied.

"Should she not be entitled to a harem as well as he?"

They hesitated but answered, "Yes."

"You then, shall be my harem," said I, rising.

"You, Cassim, shall be lord of the lips."

The polite young officer set the example of devotion by coming to my side and kissing the lips that I had committed to his charge.

"You, Selim, are the lord of the bosom."

He came up on the other side of me and kissed the bosom which peeped out above the lace front of my bodice.

"You, Rudolf, shall be the lord of the thighs."

He knelt before me, and, raising my skins, planted a kiss on the hairy mouth they concealed. Then I felt his tongue penetrate the lips beneath; it caused a flush of desire to mantle through my frame.

"Let us divest ourselves of this clothing which makes mortals of us and become like the ancient gods," I said.

My example, together with the champagne, now broke down all reserve. We stripped entirely naked and amused ourselves by imitating the attitudes usually given by art to the most celebrated heathen divinities. It was not enough for me to compare the forms of the young men by observation. I freely caressed and handled their genitals with my hands until they lost all restraint and gathered so closely about me that I was squeezed in their joint embrace.

I flung my arms around Cassim and bid him lie down on his back with me on top of him; his loins were elevated higher than his head by the pillows on which he lay. I worked backward while he guided his shaft completely into me. My buttocks presented a fair mark for Selim, who mounted me behind and slowly worked his shaft into the same orifice that Cassim had already entered. It was the tightest kind of a fit. The first entrance had stirred my desire to a flame and made me welcome the second with great greediness. Cassim's position was such that he could hardly stir, but Selim plunged his long and slender shaft into me again and again with thrusts that required all his strength. My sheath was stretched to its utmost tension by the two shafts, but all its distended nerves quivered with lust.

Rudolf now knelt close in front of me, with his knees on either side of my head. I lay for a moment with my flushed cheeks on his genitals, then I grasped his shaft in my hand and played rapidly up and down it. Cassim, with his arms wrapped around my waist, was sucking my bosoms. Selim squeezed my thighs in his grasp at every thrust he gave. I felt my crisis coming, overwhelming in three-fold intensity. In very wild abandonment I sucked Rudolf's crest in my mouth, then I thrilled and melted with a groan which resounded through all the room.

All three of the young men followed me to the realms of bliss where I soared. My sheath was overflowing with the double tribute which jetted and spurted and gushed into it. My mouth was filled with Rudolf's sperm. Both pairs of my lips were dripping. My whole frame seemed saturated with the fecund moisture. When the mingled sighs of the young men, which echoed to my prolonged groans of rapture, had died away, I sank into a semi-conscious state from which I did not rise that evening. It was a deep, dreamy, voluptuous repose which an occasional smarting sensation in my strained sheath did not disturb. The wine and profuse organs had done their work. The young men put me to bed and quietly dispersed. It was the only time I had my harem. The next day our troops lost a battle, the castle was taken by the enemy, and I was on my way to the slave market.

Anna finished her story. My shaft still peeped out from between her bosoms, but it was now stiff with desire. The fat Italian had aroused it to vitality, though she had failed to exact any tribute from it. My stones had again filled while I listened to the innocent Circassian's passionate tale. Still holding her between my thighs I turned so as to bring her on her back beneath me. Then, changing and adjusting my thighs between hers, I parted the fiery red hair that concealed lips equally fiery and commenced the onset. The delicious heat and moisture set the blood dancing in my veins. My crest lingered a moment at the lips, then glided past them into the clinging folds of her sheath. When I was completely entered, it gave a convulsive contraction around my shaft and Anna melted—indeed the ladies were all ripe to the melting point, while I had to meet their fresh successive ardour.

Anna became passive, but she still seemed to enjoy the deep and rapid thrusts which for several moments I continued to drive into her white loins. At every thrust I became more and more furious. I buried my hilt again and again in a vain attempt to touch her womb. I felt that if my crest could only reach so far up in her long slender person, I could consummate the exquisite connection. She seemed to divine my wish; she opened her thighs and, drawing her knees upward, wrapped her long, slender legs around my waist with a strength of which I had not thought her capable. Fixing my look on her sweet face I gave another plunge. She was so fairly exposed to my thrust that I rammed her womb clear up her belly. The sperm gushed from my crest in consecutive jets and I gave a sigh of perfect satisfaction.

I was completely exhausted; my nerveless frame stretched itself at full length upon her and I sank into a voluptuous languor that gradually turned into sleep. I slept fully an hour, the ladies told me on waking, and I felt my vigour returning. They brought me some sherbet and confections which further refreshed me; and one of them was so considerate as to point out to me where to make water. Then I heard that Anna had thrown the scarf so that it fell on the shoulders of two young girls and would not tell them which was to keep it but mischievously referred it to me. Leaving the disorder to the chapter of incidents, I begged them both to favour us with a story. It was a Portuguese girl named Virginia who began.

She was a pretty little creature not more than seventeen, and very small for that age. Her slight limbs were beautifully rounded and tapered to the cunningest little hands and feet. Her pretty bosoms, though small, were perfect hemispheres. Her hair was very dark and braided into strands which were carefully coiled up under a round comb. Her complexion was dark but her large fiery eyes indicated some northern blood. She and her little companion sat on either side of me, each encircled by one of my arms, while the story was in progress.

The Portuguese Lady's Story

My father was an English wine merchant in Lisbon and my mother was a Portuguese lady. I was the only child, but there was a little boy named Diego, two years older than myself, who came to reside with us. I subsequently found that he was the fruit of my father's amours before his marriage, but as Diego's mother was dead, my mother naturally let him have a home with us. Diego and I were the best of friends; among other amusements a favourite play with us was getting married. Diego knew enough to play this when no one was by, and always finished by getting on me. His organ could hardly get stiff enough to penetrate me, but he must have gradually obliterated all trace of a maidenhead, for I cannot remember ever having one. There was no consummation in our connections, neither of us was ripe enough for that, but there was a charm about it which made us keep it up at intervals for a year or two.

One evening Diego proposed, and I agreed, that we should postpone being together after our little ceremony of marriage until we went to bed. This occurred the day after I had first noticed the appearance of the marks of my first monthly period on my skin. Our rooms were joining and after I had got nearly asleep that night, for I had forgotten all about it, Diego came in. He crept into bed and getting on top of me inserted his organ as usual. Being both undressed it seemed much nicer than ever before, and we both explored each other's naked forms with our hands, my bosoms for the first time attracting Diego's attention; they were quite little, but it gave me as much pleasure to have them fondled and kissed as it seemed to give him to do it, for the Portuguese blood matures young.

Our lips now met with more fervour than ever before, and I began to have a feeling in my sheath. Diego's little shaft being in so still did not satisfy, and I gave a push upwards with my loins. He returned it with a thrust which felt pleasant. He kept thrusting incessantly for many minutes, and all the time it felt more delightful, yet I longed for the thrusts to become more deep and rapid.

"Isn't it splendid," I whispered, "do it harder."

"It's perfectly splendid," he answered, in a voice rendered almost inarticulate by rapture.

For two or three minutes we kept up the rapid motion and I felt Diego's shaft growing stiffer than ever before. The delight he afforded me was so exquisite that I culminated in a long, sweet, refreshing thrill. Diego must have melted at the same moment and paid the first tribute of his scanty drops. We both fairly whined with the excitement and delight of our unexpected success. The noise brought my mother to the room. She caught us lying exhausted in each other's arms. She took off her slipper and scourged Diego back into his room. Then she turned down the bedclothes and spanked my bottom thoroughly, and, having locked the door between my room and his, left me to my tumultuous reflections.

The next morning Diego was sent to Brazil. My parents at once began to look around for a suitable match for me, fearing, doubtless, that I might seek another opportunity to gratify my precocious passions. They fixed upon a young nobleman who was attracted by my father's wealth and promised him my hand. He was rather dissipated, but so were all the young men of family in Lisbon. He was quite good looking, and, though I had seen him but a few times, I looked forward to the marriage night with pleasure, for I longed for such another delightful experience as I had had with Diego. At length the bridal evening came. The ceremony was completed in the presence of many guests and was followed by dancing and the popping of champagne corks to a late hour. When the bridesmaids put me to bed I did not have to wait long for my husband. He came in somewhat under the influence of wine, hurriedly took off his clothes and hardly waited to kiss and embrace me before he exercised his marital rites. I was penetrated by a little object not as big as Diego's. Before I recovered from my surprise and disappointment he had completed his purpose and sank down beside me to sleep. I shed bitter tears of chagrin.

Several times every night for two or three weeks the same strange connection took place, differing only in that he was not every time immediately overcome with wine and sleep. Only once during that time did my constantly aroused and disappointed passions succeed in culminating quickly enough for me to melt, and that only partially. I dared not question him, for that would betray the experience I had had. One night I purposely left the lamp burning and waited for him to get off into a sound sleep. Then I turned the bedclothes down and examined his organ. It was a mere scarred remnant which had evidently been eaten away by disease. It was incapable from weakness of any excitement. No wonder it was constantly subjected to the torture of his disappointed desire! After this I shunned him as much as possible, finding no solace in his company and constantly tormented with desire.

"Oh, for an entire man," I sighed!

He took himself nearly every night to the gaming table. Early one evening he went off as usual. I retired to my bedroom and sat looking out through the window blind. Our house, like most others in Lisbon, was built in a quadrangle, the rear of which was the stable. If I sat on one side of the window I could only see one side of the stable wall, and I could only be seen from it. There was only one window in it, which served for Pedro the coachman, and he was rarely in his room. It was the fashion at that time in Lisbon to have large fine-looking Negroes for coachmen, who were admitted to many privileges, for there is no prejudice against colour in Portugal. Pedro was the most gigantic coachman in the city; indeed he was the largest well proportioned man I had ever seen in my life.

As I looked out through the blind I indistinctly saw him gazing towards my window. I at once determined to have some sport. Standing before the glass beside the window I lighted the lamp as if unconscious of observation—indeed I could not have been seen from any other quarter except Pedro's window, and that was small and higher than mine. I threw open the blind as if for air and began slowly to undress. Then I stood in my chemise and petticoat lazily brushing my hair before the glass, which displayed my naked arms and bosoms to good advantage.

Then I sat down to take off my shoes and lifted my foot to my knee for convenience in untying. My hidden observer must have seen under my petticoat up to my loins, and perhaps indeed an inch inside of them, for my legs were stretched very wide apart. I grew wanton with the thought of the influence I made by this time on his passions. If his desires were not thoroughly aroused it was no fault of mine. I stood before the glass again and let my petticoat and chemise fall to the floor, but delayed putting on my nightgown. I yawned and fondled my breasts with my hands as a woman does, giving as I did so an undulating motion to my loins. Soon I heard a soft and heavy tread coming from the coach room stairs towards my door. I might have locked it but I did not. Was this not just what I had been praying for? The door opened and Pedro entered. I held up my nightgown before my naked form.

"If I am too bold," he said, in great agitation, "bid me go and I will cast myself in the Tagus."

He need not have been half so tragic.

"Pedro," said I, "have you no more politeness than to keep your clothes on when a lady's undressed?"

His anxious countenance relaxed at once into a reassured smile. He gallantly kissed my hand—my lips he did not presume to kiss at all—and then undressed himself without stopping till his Herculean form stood entirely naked before me in all its gigantic but complete proportions. His immense shaft was proudly erect and huge even for such a giant. Pendant from it hung stones which seemed to my somewhat startled eyes as large as a coconut. He lifted me without an effort till my bosoms were opposite his mouth, into which he almost entirely sucked one of them. My legs wound themselves around his waist and I found myself sitting on the crest of his great stiff shaft, which was so directly underneath the lips of my sheath that it slowly entered them.

At last I was penetrated by an organ which I could hardly accommodate; the effort to do so, however, was attended with the extremest pleasure. I relaxed my legs and suffered myself to settle down with all my weight upon it till I thought his whole shaft must have entered. Then I looked in the mirror before which we were standing. At least half his great shaft was plainly visible below my buttocks. He appeared like a great statue of ebony bearing at his bosom one of ivory. I worked my loins, and I could see plainly by the mirror that his shaft was now further entered by the motion, but I had so much of it in me that I was progressing rapidly to a blissful consummation.

At this moment he laid me upon my back on the bed without losing our connection and, bracing his feet upon the footboard, gave an irresistible plunge. It seemed to ram my womb clear under my bosoms. My whole body seemed only a sheath quivering with lascivious gratification. I bore without flinching two more such plunges and then came the overwhelming thrill. In the midst of it I felt the gushing sperm spurting like a fountain in my belly. We subsided simultaneously with a long-drawn breath and Pedro at once considerately relieved me of his great weight. Twice more before he left I was spurred on by desire to court the brunt of his tremendous onset; then I made him go. I was completely gorged and sated. Three days afterwards we had to fly together to escape the imminent discovery threatened by my maid. We safely reached the African coast.

When the pretty little Portuguese finished her story I exchanged kisses with her and with her companion on the other side of me. My crest was rising, but another story would give it time to be fully ready. "My friend's name is Myrzella and she is a Persian," said Virginia, receiving another kiss for her information. Myrzella of course was kissed when she was thus named. She was younger than Virginia. The pink slit between her thighs was set off by the faintest trace of hair; it looked like a delicate sea-shell. She was quite plump. Her thighs were nearly twice the size of Virginia's. Her bosoms were developed as much as those of a northern girl several years later in life. Her hair was black and glossy as a raven's wing; it descended in two large braids to the calves of her legs when she stood erect. Her eyes were as black as her hair, large and sparkling, but full of tenderness. Her cheeks had little colour, except under emotion, but her lips were crimson red.

The Persian Lady's Story

My home, till two months ago, was on the banks of the Tigris. I was captured by Turks when on a journey to meet my affianced husband, whom I had never seen. Our party was on horseback proceeding along the bank of the river when the Turkish bandits pounced upon us. There was a flash of sabres and a volley of pistol shots which dispersed my friends, and my horse was seized by the bridle and hurried to the bank of the river. There was a boat in waiting which conveyed us over to the Turkish shore.

I soon found myself an inmate of the harem of the fierce bandit who had captured me. There were four other women in the harem among whom I was allowed to rest and refresh myself with supper, though I could eat but little. The Turk then came into the apartment. He was a man of middle age on whose countenance was written the most brutal passions. I fairly loathed the sight of him and hoped I would soon be ransomed. He put his arm around me and attempted to kiss me, but I shrank from his embrace.

"She would prefer to have you undress her," he said to the women, who seemed to enjoy the spectacle of seeing me unwillingly exposed.

They soon took everything off me but my chemise while the Turk himself stripped perfectly naked, and for the first time and under such uncongenial circumstances I saw the genitals of a man. They were excited by lust to a size which added to my plight. He again tried to take me in his arms, but I struggled so that my chemise was torn off and I cowered naked on the floor. He bid the women hold me. Each of my feet and each of my hands was seized by one of the four and I lay on my back with my arms and legs stretched apart panting from my struggles. He got upon me and entered me with one fierce and brutal thrust which tore away my maidenhead with a pang of excruciating agony. With a tremendous effort I got my hand loose from one of the women who held it and seized the Turk's dagger which lay near upon the pile of clothing he had taken off. The women all let go of me and the Turk jumped off before he had time to repeat his thrust. I sprang to the corner of the room in an agony of shame and rage, ready to kill the first who touched me. The Turk stood grasping his stiff shaft all stained with my blood; his baffled lust sought the first object on which to vent itself.

"Lie down, Achmet," he said, "I must have a tight place to finish what I have begun on that girl."

The person addressed lay belly downward and then the Turk turned up the female petticoats which had heretofore concealed the male sex of the wearer. It was indeed a boy, doubtless a eunuch whom the Turk kept to supplement the services of the three women of his harem. On the prostrate form of this boy the Turk mounted, and the grunts of satisfaction soon proclaimed that he had satisfied his brutal lust. I thanked heaven that I had not suffered him to gender with me. After awhile he arose and pulled down the petticoat over the boy's buttocks so that he again appeared in the semblance of a woman.

"Lock up that little tigercat in a room by herself," said the Turk, pointing to me.

I was glad to be alone and went into the room indicated without any opposition. I looked around for something to put on. The only article I could see was a rich suit of boy's clothing which doubtless belonged to the one in the next room. I dressed myself in these, completing my disguise by concealing my hair under the boy's turban. Then I looked from the window to see what were the chances of escape. Though I was on the second storey, it was not very high from the ground. I leapt. Then I made my way to the river and jumped into a boat that was moored at the bank. Casting it loose I floated down the stream. The night was very dark and my boat was nearly run down by a passing vessel, but I called loudly for aid and was taken on board.

Then I breathed free.

The vessel sailed down the Persian Gulf, and, crossing over to the Red Sea, proceeded to Egypt. I found my way to Alexandria in company with some merchants, one of whom took a fancy to me and engaged me as an attendant. He was trading between Alexandria and Morocco and owned the ship on which we sailed from the former port. We were the only occupants of the cabin. He was a handsome young man and he won my heart by his uniform kindness, but I did not reveal the secret of my sex.

The day before we reached Morocco, he called me into his cabin to assist him in a bath. He stripped unconcernedly before me; his form was manly and graceful but I was fascinated with the organs peculiar to his sex. They hung drooping at his loins, unconscious that a woman was looking at them—nay, touching them, for I contrived to touch them as often as I could while I bathed him. When I had finished sponging him he lay extended on the sofa for me to rub him dry. My hands explored all parts of his person, but lingered longest at his thighs—so much so that his shaft began to rise at the friction.

"Take care, little fellow," said he, "you will arouse a passion which you cannot gratify."

I felt my cheeks burning, a soft desire came through my veins and I was about to open my bosom and reveal my sex—but the thought of the terrible pang in the Turkish harem restrained me. I stooped and kissed his thighs; my cheeks brushed his genitals. Then I sat down and watched him while he dressed until the object which had so attracted me was concealed by his clothes. The next day we were in port and a dour Pasha Abdallah came on board. When his business was finished, conversation turned on me.

"I will make you a present of him," said the young merchant. "Poor little fellow! It is too bad to keep him at sea."

He did not know how dejected I looked at this change of masters, but it was no time for explanations. Abdallah took me with him and entrusted me to his chief eunuch to whom I sought the first opportunity of confiding my sex and misfortune. I have now been with these amiable people a week, but the Pasha has not touched me yet. I suppose I owe my exemption to the fact I am not a virgin.

B ut you are to all intents and purposes a virgin, my charming Myrzella," said I, tightening my arm around her waist and kissing her as she finished speaking.

She eluded my grasp and seized Virginia by the hands.

"Come," she said, "let's have a waltz."

The two pretty little creatures floated round and round the room in each other's arms, while Inez took up a lute and played a suitable accompaniment. Virginia, at every complete turn of the dance, held Myrzella in a close grasp, and their loins were pressed together. This wanton motion was kept up till their already excited passions were completely aroused. They suddenly finished the dance and lay on the cushions in each other's embrace with their thighs locked so that the lips between them were pressed together. Not only were the lips at their loins kissing, but their mouths were also glued together in this barren embrace.

I was on top of them both in a twinkling, and guided my stiff shaft between them. My nap after Anna's exhaustive embrace had restored my vigour. The stories of the young girls had aroused my passions. The thought of conferring on Myrzella her first rapture made me feel like a war horse going to battle. My shaft glided between them entering neither, but it was deliciously moistened with the dewy lips at the loins of both. As I gave another thrust Virginia slyly put her hand behind her and guided it into her own sheath. She was on top of Myrzella, between whom and myself she was pinioned. My loins were no sooner crushed against her little buttocks than I felt my crest bathed in her melting shower. To me the sensation was exquisite; to her it was final. She sank with a long-drawn sigh, perfectly limp on top of Myrzella.

I drew out my shaft and plunged it all dripping with Virginia's moisture into the pretty Persian girl. Moist as it was, it entered with difficulty the orifice which was so tight, but it entered to the hilt. Virginia's thin buttocks were but little in the way. My hand could fondle with both their bosoms at once. My crest, vivified with the moisture of them both, was battering at Myrzella's womb; my kisses were showered on the neck of one and then the other. I was transported with a double rapture which my overwrought nerves could endure no longer, and the gushing sperm came blissfully to a termination. While it was gushing the pretty Persian melted with a thrill at her first rapture. Her screams of delight were so loud and prolonged that the ladies had to hush her for fear it would alarm the guards at the gates.

I had just strength to turn Virginia over on her back close beside Myrzella. Then clasping them both in my arms, I stretched a leg between the thighs of each and we lay in a voluptuous repose, my forehead resting on the cushion and each appropriating one of my cheeks for kisses.

"Do tell us how your maidenhead was taken, Captain," said one of the ladies after I had recovered from the exhaustion of my double embrace.

"Sure enough, why not?" they cried in chorus.

So, settling myself into a luxurious position more convenient for storytelling and still clasped in the arms of Virginia and Myrzella, I began.

The Captain's First Story

When I was a boy there was a beautiful girl named Rosamond whose family estate in Yorkshire adjoined our own. Though she was some years older than I, a close but innocent feeling sprang up between us. I was her companion in horseback rides, nutting excursions and country pleasures. This intimacy was kept up till suitors began to appear for her hand, and to one of these she was finally married and went to live in London. Soon after, I was sent away to school. Rosamond, who had now been married some time, kept a standing invitation for me to visit her.

Accordingly I stopped at her house one night on my road through London. Her husband was away and we had full leisure to talk over old times. She had now expanded into an elegant woman with a form well developed and was a fine type of blonde, rosy-cheeked, blue eyed English matron. My boyish admiration grew more confirmed than ever. After dinner was over and we were sitting on the sofa together we grew so confidential that she at last unfolded her troubles to me. Her husband, she said, was unfaithful; he had even then left the city so that he might be with another woman. It was probably the first occasion on which she had confided her troubles to anyone. I hardly understood what she meant. I was as green and innocent as it was possible for a country boy to be, but when I saw her tears I knew she was unhappy and I drew her head to my shoulder and kissed her.

"Do let me console you," I said.

My meaning was innocent but she took it otherwise, I know, for the crimson mantled over her neck and cheeks. She seemed to come to some sudden determination, for she returned my caresses and kisses again and again. It was bedtime; the servants had retired. Rosamond began slowly to loosen her dress at the neck, as if making what preparations she might downstairs before retiring. I got a glimpse of two plump, white bosoms. Little more was said. We both sat deeply thinking; my thoughts were still innocent. Then she drew up her skirts as ladies sometimes do before retiring and warmed her ankles at the fire. I got a glimpse of two plump calves that were twice as big as when we used to romp through the woods in the country, but I sat profoundly still.

"George," she said, at length rising, "I feel lonesome tonight and you may sleep with me if you will."

"If you will not tell on me," said I, thinking I was too big a boy to sleep with a woman any more.

"You can trust me for that," she replied, and led the way upstairs.

I told her I thought I would undress in my own room, which I did and then sheepishly came and got into bed with her. She received me in a close embrace; my frame was clasped in her soft, white arms. Two thicknesses of linen only separated it from her glowing form and our lips met in a long, delicious kiss.

Then, for the first time, desire shot through my marrow and I felt my shaft stiffen against her belly. I knew now what she wanted. What a triumph it would be to gratify her and mingle my thin blood with the beautiful woman in my embrace, for such was my ignorant idea of the sexual connection; but to mingle with her, to pour my whole being into her was what nature impetuously demanded of me. I no longer hesitated to lift her chemise and get on top of her. My naked loins sank between her naked thighs; my face was buried in her bosoms. How it got in I do not know, but my shaft was taken in to the hilt with a sensation more sweet than had ever entered my imagination to conceive. I tried to get it in deeper; there was plenty of depth unsounded, but, though she helped me with her clasped arms, it would reach no further. I pushed and pushed with all my might to do something, I knew not what, when Rosamond gave a deep sigh and lay perfectly still.

"Have I hurt you, dear Rosamond?" I anxiously asked.

She burst into a merry laugh.

"Get off for a while," she said, "and let us rest."

I did not want to get off at all, but I did so and lay by her side with my moist and rigid shaft squeezed up against her plump thigh. It was half an hour before she would let me get in again. I spent the time in passionately kissing her cheeks, lips and bosoms and exploring all the secrets of her person with my hands. She gave the signal by partially lifting me, and again I sank upon her voluptuous form. My shaft was engulfed at the first thrust, I rapidly plunged it in again and again, now guiding it against one side and then against the other side of her gaping sheath. The heat and the moisture were more delicious than before. I felt something leaving my loins; it jetted from my crest and was lost in the profuse moisture that rose up in Rosamond. I gave a groan of ecstasy which explained to me the deep sighs she again heaved, and then I knew no more. When I became conscious again she was standing over me sprinkling water in my face.

"How you have frightened me," she said. "You lay so still and you looked so pale."

"I only want to lie quiet in your arms," I said.

She folded me tenderly in her arms and I went directly to sleep with my head pillowed on her bosom and my hand between her thighs. We were virtuous next morning. She had plucked the fruit before it was ripe and none had grown in the night to replace it. My shaft would not stiffen at the bidding of her warmest kisses. After breakfast the coach drove up for me and I went off to school. I visited Rosamond's house many times after that but she never again would allow me to take the slightest liberty with her, not even a kiss at meeting or parting. Her husband had reformed and she had no more wrongs to goad her into retaliation.

I think," said Inez, "it was a shame for a married woman to seduce an innocent boy."

"How nice it must have been," said Anna, "to take a sweet young fellow's maidenhead."

"Do tell another story, Captain," said Helene.

"Do," echoed all the others.

THE CAPTAIN'S SECOND STORY

When I arrived at the age of sixteen I was still a slender stripling, but, having an intrigue with a lady's maid, I fancied myself quite a man of the world. One evening I attended the theatre with several other young noblemen. The character of Cleopatra was splendidly sustained by an actress of Irish birth whom I will call Charlotte. She was of colossal size, but of perfect proportions. The dark complexion of her lovely face made her a good representation of the Egyptian queen, whose voluptuous person and amorous nature she delineated so finely that every man in the house was carried away; yet this magnificent woman was nearly fifty. Her powerful constitution had triumphed over time.

After the play was over we went into the green room and I was introduced to her. The charm of her person and form lost nothing on a near approach, though I detected one or two silver threads in her glossy hair. Her eyes had the brilliant sparkle of youth, her lips were plump and red and her teeth were as white as pearls. As soon as she heard my name she manifested deep interest; a tender light came into her eyes and the colour heightened in her cheeks as she began to talk of my father. Now I had heard of the trouble my father gave his friends in his youth by his infatuation for an actress. I could no longer doubt that she stood before me. Charlotte's name was free from scandal—remarkably so for an actress. Perhaps her liaison with my father had been her only folly.

"Do give a little supper party after the theatre which will meet in my room," she asked me.

I promised to do so, and accordingly met there a few actors and patrons of the theatre. We had a modest supper where wit, not wine, reigned. I sat next to Charlotte who seemed hardly able to take her eyes off me.

When the guests rose to go, I lingered at the door, and they went without noticing that I remained. The impulse was mutual to clasp each other in our arms.

"Oh, how I wish that you had been my son! It ought to have been so."

I was in no mood to be made a baby of. The grand voluptuous form of the queenly actress aroused far other emotions when it was folded to mine.

"Is this your bedroom?" said I, drawing her towards the door.

"For shame, Georgie," she said, as a crimson blush spread from her cheeks to her splendid bosoms. She was in the costume of Cleopatra, over which she had thrown a long mantle after the play. This mantle had fallen off. It was evident that she had intended no assignation for she moved reluctantly to the door—but she returned the passionate kiss I planted full on her mouth. So commanding was her height that she had to stoop slightly to do it. As soon as we entered the bedroom she sat down on the bed and covered her face with her hands. I took the opportunity to divest myself of most of my clothes and then I stole up to her and kissed her naked and massive shoulder. She rose to her feet and, taking me in her strong arms as if I were an infant, she walked back and forth across the room with me.

"Oh! Georgie, Georgie," she cried. "This is almost incest, but I can deny you nothing—I, who have allowed no man to embrace me since those delicious days of long ago."

She still carried me in her arms, walking to and fro. My face was in contact with her great bosoms, each of which was as large as my head. As I passionately kissed them, my right hand dropped to her thighs, from which it parted the loose oriental drapery and found in it a shaggy mass of curls. Searching to the bottom of these it found a pair of moist, warm lips. I lifted my face from her bosom to meet hers and we exchanged a kiss. It differed from those she had heretofore given me. It was as voluptuous as my own and was prolonged until I felt her other lips, which my hand was searching, begin to swell and grow hot. Charlotte carried me rapidly to the bed. Her mood was changed from maternal tenderness to fiery passion.

She laid me upon my back and sprang upon me. She folded me in her great muscular arms; her ponderous thighs settled on my own. Immense as they were, they were as a young girl's. It was her hand which guided my rigid shaft amid the thick profusion of hair till it was fairly entered and rammed to the hilt by the vibration of her powerful loins. So firmly was I pinned to the bed by her great weight that I could not move. I felt as if I were about to be ravished like a woman. It was a novel sensation and charming as it was novel. Charlotte suddenly turned over on her back without relaxing her hold in the least upon me. I found myself on top of her, but she was still master of the situation. Her arms and legs were wrapped so tight around me that my bones fairly cracked. It was the rapid undulation of her loins alone that moved our closely joined forms. Her mouth was fastened on mine as if she was about to devour me; her big womb pressed against my crest. I felt the crisis coming overwhelmingly in the powerful embrace in which I was held.

At this moment her muscles began to relax with her profuse melting shower. I spent, not with a stinted jet, but with profuse gushes that made a suitable tribute to the magnetism of her massive beauty. The rapture lasted me some time, even after I became nerveless, and at length died imperceptibly away.

"Now, you must go, you naughty boy," said Charlotte tenderly, kissing and spanking me.

"In ten minutes more my maid will come to undress me."

I was scarcely able to rise from her arms after such a long and exhausting orgasm. I was like a squeezed and sucked orange; my vigour was all gone. It was fortunate that my ship was to sail the next day—I was a midshipman under my first orders and I had to go. If the intrigue had been pursued it would have ruined her reputation and my health.

A nd now, Captain, tell us another," was the persistent petition of all the ladies, and I complied.

THE CAPTAIN'S THIRD STORY

After I had grown to manhood, I was one summer at a place of public resort in the highlands of Scotland. One night after I had gone to bed I heard voices close beside me. Then I noticed that my head lay close to a door which separated my room from the one adjoining it. The voices were evidently those of a young married couple in bed and, like myself, close to the door which separated my room from theirs. I heard kisses and then a sound as if the lady's buttocks were being spanked. Then there was a struggle, and then the young man's voice said in a coaxing tone, "Please, dear Alice, do let me."

"No, Charlie, you ought to be ashamed of yourself. I am right in the midst of my period and I have been bleeding all day. Wait till you come next week and you shall have some, and be sure and bring some condoms with you. There are none left and it would be dreadful to make a baby so soon. Now lie on your side of the bed and go to sleep—don't squeeze my thighs that way; it only makes you worse."

The sweet voice of Alice grew increasingly angry.

I heard Charlie turn over and they both soon went to sleep. My passions were aroused and my shaft grew rigid, but I lay perfectly quiet during the conversation so as to keep them in ignorance that they had a listener. The next morning they were near me at the breakfast table. Alice was a little blonde, the smallest and youngest bride I ever saw in Great Britain. She was so slender and had such large innocent blue eyes that she looked like a child in woman's dress. Charlie was a young surgeon; he was about my own age and his size and appearance resembled my own.

After breakfast he started for Edinburgh, where he practised through the week, returning to his bride to pass Sundays. During his absence I paid assiduous attention to Alice, hoping to engage her in an intrigue. She was a lively little thing, but her life was all for Charlie, with whom I could see she was yet deeply in love. I became enamoured of her artless beauty. I longed to possess her, if only for one embrace. Her indifference only made me long for her more madly. All the week I went to bed with a stiff and hot shaft, close to the little beauty but unknown to her. Saturday night brought Charlie, all radiant with the promise I had overheard Alice make him the week before. I sat in my room reading when at early bedtime they came to their room. The kisses they exchanged when the door was shut were very aggravating to me. My shaft became perfectly rigid. Just at this moment there came a call for Charlie to go to a neighboring hamlet to set a broken limb; with a muttered curse he reluctantly obeyed the call.

I knew it would take him three hours at least. I listened to Alice undressing; then I heard the tinkle of a little stream of water in crockery; then she put out the light and went to bed. Night after night the little bride had gone to sleep unconscious that she was near me, and now was once more asleep as I could hear from her regular breathing—but tonight her door was unlocked, waiting for Charlie. Would it be possible for me to impersonate him? The risk would be a terrible one, but the rigidity of my shaft put an end to reason and conscience. If I could fill those graceful little loins of hers the world might come to an end for all I cared. I stole softly in my shirt and drawers out into the corridor and into Alice's room. I crept carefully into bed with her and took her in my arms. I caressed her cunning round bosoms and felt her plump and polished thighs. They were much larger than I had imagined they were seeing her dressed. She had a few little curls between them, which I was daintily fingering when she woke up.

"So you have come, Charlie," she said.

For reply I fastened my mouth to hers and we continued uninterruptedly to exchange kisses. She was honestly ready to give Charlie what she had promised him. She opened her legs for the expected charge and I did not disappoint her. My crest entered the delicious tightness.

"What a great clumsy condom you have on," she said.

From this I inferred that my naked shaft was much bigger than Charlie's with condom on. I gave a plunge that drove my crest far in among the quivering membranes, far up in her loins. I was in rapture. The burning moments repaid me for my longing—and for any possible retribution to come. She enjoyed it as much as I did, judging from the increased ardour of knees and the motion of her thighs. I gave another plunge so deep mat my shaft seemed to disturb her slender waist and my crest to up heave her bosom.

"Oh, Charlie," she said, with a dying sigh.

Another plunge and the sheath of the young bride was flooded with mingled gushes. A moment of perfect stillness followed. To me it was a moment of ineffable satisfaction and perfect bliss. Then she suddenly scrambled from beneath me.

"The condom must have burst!" she said, hastily pouring water into me basin and washing herself. Pretty soon she came back to bed and nestled in my arms. I pretended to be overcome with drowsiness and languor and answered two or three of her questions with an inarticulate, "Eh?" The completeness with which she had melted was soon evident from the deep sleep of exhaustion into which she sank. Then I stole silently from her bed back into my own, but did not go to sleep. I awaited anxiously Charlie's return. In due time he came. While he was undressing, Alice awoke. I heard her ask him drowsily, "Why did you go out?" meaning why had he got up and gone out, after he had returned to bed with her.

"I had to go out," he replied, meaning he had had to go and attend a professional call.

She must have thought he had a necessary occasion to go into the yard. I heard her yawn and turn over as he got into bed with her and then the more significant sound of the creaking of the bed which made me more jealous. This was followed by Charlie's deep sigh; then all was still save the regular breathing of the two sleepers. It made me happy to think Alice had not joined in the sighing. I believe this gave me more pleasure than my successful escape from discovery. The next morning at breakfast Alice looked me right in the eye with her large, innocent eyes, perfectly unconscious that but a few hours before she had rapturously melted in my arms.

What a shame!" said Inez.

"There was no harm done after all," said Anna.

"Well, then," said I, "listen to another story. Perhaps this will please you all."

THE CAPTAIN'S FOURTH STORY

During one of my stays in port, my uncle, who was a member of the ministry, needed a confidential messenger to one of the German courts. I accepted the mission with pleasure. The business took me but a few days, during which I mingled in the festivities of the court. The sovereign was very gracious to me; his spouse I did not see, though it was said she was in the gallery of the dining hall during one of the state dinners at which I was present. It was known to all when I was to return and on the evening before I started I had declined several invitations that I might get ready to go. Just at nightfall I received the following singular note: A lady sends her compliments to Lord George Herbert and begs that he will call at No. 300,—Street.

I hesitated what to do all the time I was enjoying my after-dinner cigar, but I finally put a pistol in my pocket and proceeded to the place named. It was a neat house in a respectable street. I was received at the door by a nice elderly lady and ushered into a well but plainly furnished room. She thanked me for being so kind as to come.

"I have received you at the door myself," she said, "because I thought best to have my servant away. It is a strange request I have to make of you, but your reputation for gallantry is known to me. May I rely on your honour to keep it secret, whether you grant it or not?"

I assured her she might.

"My foster daughter, whom I dearly love," she said, "is married, but the union has not been blest with children. Her husband is very desirous of having an heir. He blames her very unjustly and is making her life wretched, for she loves him. She can endure his reproaches no longer. I have known it was not her fault and I have advised her to do what necessary to get an heir. Now, my lord, have I advised her rightly?"

"Perhaps so," said I, "but what have I got to do with it? I am about to leave this city tomorrow, probably never to see it again."

"That is the very reason," she said, "that I have invited you to come here to meet her. She has seen you and wishes that heir to inherit your noble blood and handsome person and, this once accomplished, never to see or be seen by its sire for the desire for an heir and not wantonness has influenced her. Do you consent?"

"I must see the lady," I replied.

"She would die of mortification if you should see her and reject her," said the old lady, "but there is no fear of that. If you are pleased with her, go up and kiss her hand when I present you."

She then conducted me upstairs and open the chamber door. A lady was standing in the centre of the room looking timidly at me as I entered. As soon as I saw the lady I loosened my grasp on the pistol which I had in my pocket. All fear of treachery vanished from my mind and another sentiment immediately took its place. I approached her and kissed her hand. The old lady shut the door and retired. I was alone with a woman not in fact beautiful, but very interesting. Her figure was fine and her features, though irregular, were pleasing. Her look fell to the carpet; the ensign of modesty warmed on her cheeks, receded and paled, then showed again more rosy than before. Her hand trembled in mine. Her attire made no accession to her appearance. She was dressed in plain muslin without an ornament and her hair was plainly brushed; but there was that in her air which convinced me that she was a lady, and that too in an embarrassing position.

"Fair lady," said I, "your choice has fallen on one who can appreciate your delicacy, notwithstanding the strange circumstances which brought you to this."

A grateful smile lighted for an instant her fine face, but she involuntarily averted her cheek from the kiss I pressed upon it. She did not reply, nor did she speak once during the whole interview. By this time I felt that the task of getting her with child would be the most agreeable one that had ever fallen to my lot to perform. She stood passive in a deep reverie, looking almost unconscious while I unfastened her dress and let it fall to the floor. Her undergarments were of the finest lawn and lace. The stud that fastened her chemise was a large diamond, which only confirmed my opinion she was a lady of high station. I kissed her beautiful white bosoms which were now disclosed. She awoke from her reverie with another deep blush and, going to the other side of the bed, she took off her shoes with her back to me, so that I did not get a glimpse of one finely turned ankle. Then she dropped off her petticoat and got into bed, covering herself up, face and all. I soon undressed and followed.

I took her in my arms and kissed her tenderly. Though she suffered my lips to revel on her ripe mouth, her lips did not move to return my kisses. My hands wandered over all parts of her fine form. As long as they lingered on her bosoms she was passive, but when I played too wantonly with the curls at her loins, she grew restless. I was excited by her modesty to the highest pitch of desire. I drew her unresisting form beneath me and, parting her thighs, my crest entered the Elysian Fields—indeed the promised joy of the Elysian Fields would not have tempted me to withdraw it. It entered where it was surrounded by moist, clinging tissues alive with affinity to its sensitive touch. Still she lay passive. I put my arms under the small of her back and, holding her firmly, gave a plunge which sent my crest until it touched her womb. She could no longer refrain from manifesting her delight; she wrapped her arms around me.

I gave another thrust which unsealed the fountain of my glans, and then another which planted the gushing sperm in the midst of her loins. She held my face between her hands and gazed entranced with her eyes while the life-giving fluid dashed against her womb. She melted while she gazed and put up her lips for the first and only kiss she exchanged with me. Our lips were glued together till the last drop trickled from my crest, and the thrilling rapture slowly faded and left me nearly lifeless in her arms. The life which she had ravished from me could hardly fail to quicken in her womb, and her melting gaze as she reviewed them could hardly fail to stamp the nascent life with my features. We lay perfectly still for a long time; then the door opened and the old lady called me. I got up to see what she wanted.

"You must go now," she said. I told her I could not bear to leave my charming companion.

"You will undo what I hope you have done if you stay longer."

Then she whispered, "I do not wish to startle her, but there is danger of discovery. Lie perfectly still on your back, darling," she added to the lady in bed, "and it will be a fine boy."

I dressed and stepped to the bedside. The sheet was drawn; her forehead alone was visible. I kissed it and withdrew. The old lady soon followed me and put a ring into my hand as she dismissed me hastily from the front door.

"She begs you to accept it in token of her admiration and respect. Her love is all for her husband."

I should not have accepted it if I had seen, as I did on reaching home, that it was a diamond worth thousands. On the inside of the ring were engraved the words, IN HONOUR. . . I left the city, as had been announced, on the fist morning train. Before proceeding far we met with an accident. No one was injured, but we would have to wait for the afternoon train. I took a carriage and rode back to the city rather than kick my heels. As we approached the main street we could not cross.

We had to pause, to allow the cortege of the sovereign to pass. By his side was sitting his august spouse. It was the lady with whom I had lain the night before. She supposed me far on my journey or she would not have left the seclusion of her palace. She rode unconscious of the presence of the man whose seed was even then germinating in her womb. It is six months since then. The newspapers which we received at port a few days ago announce that there is great rejoicing in a certain capital city. The august spouse of the sovereign is in an interesting condition.

You see what you have got to expect, Inez," said Anna. "You, I and Myrzella. What will the black-eyed Pasha say if three blue-eyed babies are born the same night in the harem?"

The ladies laughed and then began teasing for another story.

"One of you must tell it then," said I.

When they found that I would tell no more, enquiries were made for the scarf. Virginia produced it and threw it to a lady she called El Jelis, from Arabia. She, like Anna, was very tall and slender, but there all resemblance between them ceased. The Arab girl had hair and eyes as black as jet, and skin the colour of rich cream. She took the scarf and shook it out to its full length, displaying the spots where Zuleika's blood had stained it.

"You will excuse me if I give you a dance instead of a story," she said, springing lightly to her feet and waving the long thin fabric high over her head.

She accompanied the waving motion with the most beautiful dancing I ever saw. Her slender but firmly rounded limbs seemed to float through the air. Her little feet came to the carpet with a touch too light to crush a rose petal. Her shining black hair was unbound and reached to her ankles; it floated from side to side as she danced like a cloud. Her motion without losing its grace became more rapid; the colour came to her cheeks; her large, lustrous, black eyes flashed from under the dark lashes. Still the dance became more rapid.

Her round bosoms did not even quiver, so free from any jar was every graceful spring. At last her whole form seemed to float in the air, then one toe lightly touched the carpet and the other pointed to the ceiling directly over her head. For an instant between her naked thighs was disclosed a long, crimson gash and the parted curls. In another instant she was standing upright and motionless before me. Her hands were folded on her bosoms and her head bowed in oriental submission. Her hair slowly ceased to wave and fell to her ankles in a veil.

"It was very graceful, my charming El Jelis," said I, "but I cannot let you off from your story."

"My story is so disgraceful that I cannot look you in the face and tell it," she said and, turning with her back towards me, the beautiful girl told the following story.

The Arabian Lady's Story

I was born in the dominions of the Imam of Yemen. When I was sixteen years old I was selected by one of his emissaries for the Imam's harem. My parents were well pleased with my preferment, and I set out from home with girlish glee. On being introduced to the harem I was bathed and elegantly dressed; then I was led to a room where the Imam was sitting conversing with his ladies. He was an old man with a countenance indicating a feeble character. The conversation showed the supremacy which was exercised over him by his wife, Ayesha, a very fat lady, whose corpulence seemed to be her only charm. After a while the Imam began to look at me a great deal, which I could see she noticed.

At last he called me to his side, where I stood with his bare arm around my waist, answering his questions. His arm gradually lowered and I felt his hand under my petticoat. I suppose he thought the other ladies did not see him, for I was standing very close to his side. The eyes of Ayesha, however, were on the alert; they flashed with anger. The Imam's hand explored my thighs, and at last his finger entered a place where no man had ever before touched me. It felt its way carefully in and soon met with an obstruction. The pressure upon it, though slight, was very disagreeable to me, but I did not dare to repulse the Imam. What I did not dare to do Ayesha did.

"Your Highness," said she, "has promised to present a virgin to the Sultan of Muscat; I think this one will do in default of any better."

"Yes, she is a virgin," he said, partly answering her and partly giving vent to his own thoughts.

"Shall I order the chief eunuch to see to her?" said Ayesha.

The Imam gave a long look at me, then he looked at the black thunder cloud on the brow of Ayesha, from beneath which her eyes were flashing.

"Yes," he said, "you may give the order."

I supposed the graceful charm which rewarded his obedience was in possession of some state secret which controlled him—or it may have been her temper. The next day I was on the road to Muscat, where, after several days' journey, I was duly presented. The Sultan received his present very graciously. I heard him say a bale of rich goods should be returned to my former lord. Then he ordered the female slaves to care for me very tenderly. They bathed me and perfumed me and dressed me in the richest apparel and jewellery, then they led me to a sumptuous repast—they could not do too much for me, whom their lord delighted to honour.

After supper the Sultan came into the women's apartments. I had learned from the slave girls that Fatima was his favourite wife. She was a beautiful woman, but I found afterwards that she had a cruel and pitiless heart. She did not seem to care for the attentions the Sultan lavished on me. I even thought there was a gleam of satisfaction on her countenance as he led me to a remote part of the harem. We passed through two or three doors until nothing could be heard of the sounds of music or conversation we had just left. We were now in a rich apartment with an elegant bed. As I was somewhat agitated the Sultan sat on a sofa beside me and began to soothe me. His person was agreeable and I began to enjoy his conversation. I knew what was coming, but I neither desired nor dreaded it much.

"Now please undress yourself," he said.

I obeyed at once, taking off everything but my chemise; in the meantime he had stripped stark naked. It made my heart beat violently as I looked for the first time on a man's shaft ready for action. He came and unbuttoned my chemise and let it drop to the floor. I covered my face with my hands. He lifted me and laid my back on the bed close to the edge of it and knelt on the floor beside me. Then he spread my thighs wide apart and opened the lips between them and made a critical examination of my virginity.

"By Allah!" he exclaimed, "a crescent-shaped maidenhead. It brings good luck to the captor!"

"I am glad it pleases you, my lord," said I, timidly.

The Sultan gave a sudden cry of agony and fell across me. I took my hands from my face and saw Fatima holding a shawl tightly around his head while a man whom I had never seen was driving a dagger into his body with repeated blows. I tried to call out, but my voice was frozen with horror.

"Dare to make a noise," said Fatima, "and you shall share his fate."

I knelt to plead for my life, but they took no further notice of me till they had satisfied themselves that the Sultan was dead. Fatima flung the covers over the body.

"Let me be the first to congratulate you as Sultan of Muscat," she said, turning to her companion.

"The most beautiful woman in Muscat has the right to congratulate me," he said. Then he turned towards me, let his eyes rove over my naked form and addressed some soothing words to me.

"Have the decency to put on your clothes and follow me, hussy," said Fatima.

While I was dressing the Sultan parted with Fatima, first giving her some instructions about the harem to carry out while he went to confirm his authority with the troops. The conspiracy at the crowning act, at which I was present, was perfectly successful, and the new Sultan reigned without opposition. Fatima was absolute in the harem. She kept me as much as possible out of sight of the new Sultan, though she allowed him to have free access to the other women. He took every opportunity to speak to me, but I avoided him with horror. I could not forget the scene of the assassination.

One evening after he had been more persistent in his attentions, Fatima called me into a room alone. She told me to lie down on the bed, and, when I had obeyed her, she turned my petticoats up over my head. I was so afraid of the beautiful tigress that I dared not stir; I only begged for mercy.

"Lie still, I shall not hurt you," she said, and, having pulled my thighs apart, she opened my sheath with her fingers. I heard the "click" of scissors and felt a slight but keen pain. I put my hand involuntarily to the place and felt that my maidenhead was gone.

"Now," she said, "you will not play your arts on the Sultan any more on pretence of being a virgin."

I burst into tears of mortification and anger and went into my room with the blood trickling down my thighs. The next evening the Sultan came into the women's apartments. Fatima hastily ordered me from the room on some errand.

"Don't be too harsh with the poor maid," he said.

"Maid!" she retorted, contemptuously. "She has lain with half the young men in Yemen."

"I will match your wager on that," he said.

"Very well," she said. "If you are right you shall lie with her tonight. If I am right I will dispose of her."

This conversation was carried on in a low tone, but I overheard it. She arose and bade me follow her. The Sultan came after us to the bedroom.

"Now feel the hussy," she said, "and satisfy yourself." The Sultan, brute as he was, was very much embarrassed. But he drew me towards him, put his hands under my clothes and with his finger satisfied himself that my maidenhead was gone. I was then dismissed with my cheeks flaming with rage and shame, and then the two devils passed the night together. Once more after this the Sultan sought an opportunity to be alone with me, which I baffled. Fatima's keen eyes detected him and my fate was sealed. That evening I was seized in my room by the eunuchs, bound and gagged and sewn in a sack.

After being carried a short distance in silence, the creaking of a boat and the rippling of water revealed to me the awful doom to which I was to be consigned. I could not move; I could not call. I was lifted and flung into the water and heard a boat row away. I settled slowly under the waves, and, as my clothes became saturated, the water reached my nostrils. I made in hopeless agony a prayer to Allah; as if in answer to it I heard the stroke of oars. They became louder and louder till the water settled over me and I knew no more. I returned to consciousness lying in the bottom of a boat, the sweet moonlight streaming in my face and the eyes of a young man gazing earnestly into my own. He must have been pleased with what he saw there.

"Sweet houri of paradise, she lives," he said, in a tender and manly tone.

His attentions were unremitting until I was fully restored and my lungs freed from water. Then he arranged me in the bottom of the boat with his coat for a pillow.

"Lie close, we may be observed," he said.

He rowed silently to shore in the suburbs of the city where he had a little dwelling, which we reached without observation and to which he made me welcome. He offered me in the most delicate manner some clothing of his own until mine could be dried. Then he cooked me a nice meal, and after I was thus refreshed we conversed without reserve. He listened to my story with his face beaming with compassion; it lighted with joy when I allowed him to infer that my person as well as heart was still to be disposed of as far as any man was concerned. I emphasised man for I thought of the fiendish and jealous rape Fatima had accomplished. Hassan, for that was his name, soon told his story. He had come into the city to seek his fortune and had been driven to smuggling to obtain a livelihood. It was while on the alert at this vocation that he had been able to save me.

"We must fly before morning," he said, "if we would be safe."

He would be the happiest man in the world if I could suffer him to take me to his desert home. So much kindness after so much cruelty completely won my heart. He read my assent in my eyes and, kissing me tenderly, went out to make his preparations to go. We were soon both mounted on a single horse and miles away from Muscat. We had been an hour on the road and were still borne along at the same unflagging gallop. Hassan held me in front of him like a baby in his arms, often kissing me, his kisses constantly growing more ardent until I felt his stiff shaft pressing against my person. He suggested that I should ride astride awhile and rest myself by a change of position. I obeyed his suggestion, turning with my face towards his, putting my arms around his neck, while my thighs were wide open over Hassan's.

He let the bridle drop over the horse's neck, whose headlong pace subsided into a gentle canter which was like the rocking of a cradle. Hassan put his arm around my loins and lifted me a little; his other hand was busy clearing away the petticoats and then I felt the crest of his naked shaft knocking for entrance between my naked thighs. I was willing to yield to Hassan anything that he wished but no sooner had the lips of my sheath been penetrated than I involuntarily clung more tightly around his neck and, sustaining myself in that way, prevented him from entering further. I found the sensation entirely different, however, from that which I had experienced when the fingers of the Imam explored the same entrance. Now the organ seemed adapted to the place and excited a sensation of pleasure. I offered my mouth to Hassan and returned his ardent kisses with an ardour equally warm.

A desire to secure more of the delightful intruder overcame my dread of the intrusion. I loosened my hold on Hassan's neck and my weight drove his shaft so completely home, notwithstanding the tightness of the fit, that his crest rested on my womb. It felt so unexpectedly good that I gave a murmur of delight. The motion of the horse kept partially withdrawing and then completely sending it in again at every canter. The first thrust, good as it was, was completely eclipsed by each succeeding one. I could have murmured with delight still louder, but kept still for very shame. What would Hassan think of a girl so wanton?

But he was in no condition to think. He was fiercely squeezing and kissing me, while at every undulating motion of the cantering horse he seemed to penetrate me more deeply. The pleasure was too exquisite to be long endured. It culminated in a melting thrill, and my moisture mingled with the sperm that gushed from Hassan's crest. He reeled in the saddle but recovered himself. The cantering motion drove his shaft less deeply in as it became more limber. It finally dropped out of me, a little limp thing drowned in the descending moisture.

"What a conquest for a slender girl to achieve over such a formidable object," I thought. Exhausted, but triumphant, I dropped my head on Hassan's shoulder.

"Poor girl," said he, "how it makes you bleed!"

"Never mind," I whispered.

He always remained under this innocent delusion, for the trying scenes of that eventful night brought on my period prematurely and my petticoats before morning were stained with blood. Twice more during the night he slackened the speed of his horse, and each time we completed an embrace equally satisfactory. At dawn we were beyond the reach of pursuit, safe and free.

E l Jelis finished as she began, with her back towards me, while I was reclining against Myrzella and Virginia. The graceful Arabian was astride my thighs, partly kneeling on the carpet and partly lying on my loins. She played with my genitals all the time she was telling her story and my shaft got so stiffened that she inserted it. It was sufficiently excited to enjoy the charming retreat where it was cherished. My glands relaxed and my pendant was fondled in her tapered fingers and caressed by the soft hair which hung down from her loins. I lay luxuriously quiet, but El Jelis had been longing all the evening for the connection and she could not keep still. She made little wanton motions with her loins all the while she was speaking, and at every move the moist, warm tissues where my crest was hidden quivered with life and imparted their vitality to me.

I would have summoned energy to give her the thrusts for which she longed but I postponed it from moment to moment, revelling passively in the lascivious situation. El Jelis could no longer restrain herself. She finished her story and began to play her loins up and down my shaft, which though erect to its full size, was not entirely rigid, and it bent with her vigorous motion. Her position was favourable to the play of her loins and she moved them with greater and greater rapidity. I seemed to have changed my sex and to be a woman actually enjoying the thrusts of her paramour. In a few moments I would have been ripe to melting, but El Jelis could not wait; her buttocks settled heavily upon me, her sheath loosened and her moisture flushed my genitals. She sank back with a deep sigh into my arms, which drew my shaft completely out of her and exposed it like a tower rising tempestbeaten from the waves. It subsided at once when the stimulating efforts of El Jelis were withdrawn.

I was not ready for another onset. The ladies were too polite to laugh; I had exerted myself too much on their behalf. El Jelis threw the scarf and then nestled quietly in my arms. It fell to the ninth lady. She was a Parisian and her name was Renee. The others had done well to leave her to the last, for she was the most beautiful woman in the room. The sweetness and vivacity of her expression and the grace of her manner lent additional charm to her perfect features and her splendid form. She was of medium height with full contours, graceful as a fawn yet voluptuous in the bold roundness of her bosoms and the grand swell of her thighs. Her complexion was wonderfully clear. Her snow-white skin was so transparent that a delicate pink tinge showed plainly beneath it, especially at the little ears and the small tips of her fingers.

The rosy tinge was deep on her lips and her mouth was like an opening red rose.

Her large hazel eyes were clear and full and the long lashes that partially veiled them could not conceal their lustre. Her hair was of a dark chestnut colour, but if the light fell full upon it, it was of a golden auburn; it began to curl at the centre of her head where it was parted, and would have descended in a luxuriant mass to her knees if it had not been carefully confined by combs. The hair at her loins was dark but had a ruddy tinge. After she had exchanged a kiss with me she reclined in a graceful position at my feet where I could uninterruptedly feast my eyes on her marvellous beauty while she told her story.

THE FRENCH LADY'S STORY

When I arrived at the age of sixteen I was still at a convent boarding school in Paris. Lisette, my roommate, was my most intimate friend. I confided to her all my secrets and supposed she did the same to me, especially what we could learn about marriage and sexual intercourse, a subject which had a strange fascination, even for a girl like myself who had never engaged in it, but who looked forward to an early marriage with eager satisfaction. One evening Lisette came into the room with a triumphant expression. She had something in a small box which she mysteriously produced. It was labelled: "One Superfine Dildo".

She locked the door and, opening the box, revealed an India-rubber article about the size of a man's shaft ready for action. She explained to me what it was and said she had got it from her milliner as a great favour and had paid her five hundred francs for it. She was all eagerness to try it.

"But, Lisette," said I, "if we do, and if we should ever get married, our husbands would know it."

"Oh!" she said, "we could easily fool them."

Having filled the dildo with warm water and fastened it upon my loins with the straps attached to it, she prevailed upon me to act the man's part. She pulled me into bed and seemed perfectly familiar with the proper manner for me to mount her. So far from being hurt by the thing, Lisette seemed to enjoy every movement of it, from the time I thrust it into her till she gave a dying sigh and subsided. After a while she was ready to perform the same office for me. When she had got it adjusted I felt the warm thing enter in a little way with a sensation not unpleasant. Then she gave a thrust with all her might which tore away my maidenhead. It pained me so cruelly, that I pushed her off me and burst into tears while the blood trickled from the wound and down my thighs.

I was terribly enraged with Lisette but I finally forgave her when she told me that my brother had taken her maidenhead when she was on a visit to me. Both Lisette and myself were married soon after leaving school, she to a country gentleman and I to an officer. Lisette had not been long married when I had too good reason to suppose that she had kept up a liaison with my brother. I wrote to her hinting at my painful suspicion and begging her to make a visit that I might persuade her to break off a connection so dangerous to both herself and my brother. She replied saying that she could not visit me now, but she would be glad if I would receive a visit from her unmarried sister, adding that she was a shy, timid girl and that a visit to Paris would do her good.

Her sister Amie accordingly came in due time and was cordially welcomed by me, though I had never seen her before. She was a handsome girl, but very masculine in appearance, although she appeared to be very modest. Her features were pleasing but rather large, and though she was broad-shouldered and tall, her bosoms seemed to be flat and her thighs small. She wore her hair very short, even for the clipped style then prevailing for young ladies. My husband was at this time off with his regiment, and I thought it would be kind to allow Amie to sleep with me. When we retired she seemed to be very awkward about retiring, but finally followed me to bed. I took her in my arms and kissed her affectionately.

She returned the kisses and caresses with so much ardour that I wished Louis, my husband, was in her place. He had been absent long enough for my desires to become like tinder, ready to flame up at a spark. So we lay locked tightly in each other's embrace with our lips glued together. I felt something squeezed up against my thigh which could not be Amie's arm, for both of her arms were around me. I put my hand down and felt that it was a man's warm, throbbing shaft. I gave a scream and pushed my bedfellow violently from me.

"You are not Lisette's sister!" was my absurd exclamation.

"True, charming Renee, but I am her brother, and no one will ever know of this but her. Will you now allow Armand to have one sweet kiss like those you have just given to Amie?"

He drew me towards him as he spoke, with the fire of passion on his handsome face. I hesitated, but my sheath was still swelling with wanton emotion and I suffered him again unresisted to take me in his arms. This was not the moral lecture I had prepared for Lisette. Desire was coursing through all my veins; I returned Armand's kisses; I opened my thighs to facilitate the connection. The touch of his crest under the hair was like the first taste of some delicious fruit unexpectedly presented to the lips of a thirsty traveller. I took it in so greedily and swallowed it with a sensation so pleasurable that I was ashamed of myself.

Armand would think he was not the first who had taken advantage of my husband's absence. But I could not help it; my person had been seduced before my consent had been won. It was too late now for virtue to erect a barrier. I was penetrated to the secret and sensitive depths where wantonness reigned supreme. The rapidity and strength of Armand's thrusts showed the vigour of seventeen. I was transported to the seventh heaven, carried by the amorous boy in his arms. When I finally returned to the consciousness of earthly things we lay so still that for a few moments there was not a motion in the bed, save that Armand's diminished shaft was slowly sinking from my sheath with the balmy flow that filled it. Armand's visit was prolonged to a week and no suspicion was excited on the part of my friends and servants, nor was the intrigue known in any quarter save by Lisette, who rallied me without mercy.

It was a week of abandonment to unrestrained wantonness. I would sometimes ask Armand, when in the privacy of my room, to take his male attire from his trunk and put it on. He then seemed like a slender and effeminate youth, a mere fair-faced boy, entirely different from the Amazon he appeared in girl's clothes. But if I rallied him on his effeminacy, he would at once proceed to give most convincing proof of his virile power. No married embrace ever conferred such rapture. Fornication, that becomes so insipid when lawful, is so delicious when stolen. The lascivious nights were not enough; we retired every afternoon on the pretence of taking a nap. At every embrace his fresh enthusiasm bewitched me and I was melted by his fervent ardour. But dark and sunken circles came around Armand's eyes, his flesh fell rapidly away, and when at last he tore himself away from me to return home, a hectic fever was consuming him.

As for me, I grew plump as he grew thin, and my cheeks bloomed with stolen pleasure. When my husband returned home on leave of absence, he had no occasion to reproach me for want of ardour. Life had, however, begun to be monotonous, when we received an invitation from Lisette, seconded by her husband, Adolphe, to visit their country seat, an invitation was accepted. We sat up late the first evening. There was much to converse about, and besides, the champagne flowed freely. I enjoyed conversing with so agreeable a man as Adolphe, especially as he was fat and jolly. The change was agreeable from being continually with my husband, who was thin and earnest. Lisette and I talked on after our husbands had retired. We finished another bottle of wine, which they had merely opened, and we grew very confidential. We concluded by undressing by the stove and carrying our clothes upstairs in our hands. Standing in our chemises we compared our forms: as of old, they were very similar. We pressed our bosoms together and we squeezed together the little mouths at our loins.

"Why do we stand here," I said, "when we can go to bed and get all we want?"

"Suppose," she said, "we should make a mistake going to our rooms and exchange husbands?"

I looked at Lisette to see if she had divined my own adulterous thoughts and to see if she was really in earnest. She smiled and nodded; so did I. Wine and wantonness combined to put us up to that mad frolic. It was agreed she was to take my clothes along with her and that I should take hers with me, in case of the necessity of suddenly escaping to our own rooms. As she put her hand on the doorknob of my husband's room I felt a pang of jealousy, but I let that disappear and entered Adolphe's room. He was sleeping quietly. I laid Lisette's clothes on a chair and got into bed with him. I waited a few moments for the violent beating of my heart to still and then nestled close up and put my arms around him. I put aside his moustache and kissed him on the lips. Still he did not wake. Then I pulled up his shirt and felt his massive thighs and played with his genitals. They grew under my hand and he awoke and put his arms around me. I returned his kisses and caresses.

"Why, Lisette," he said, "how good you are tonight."

I replied with kisses. Then he got upon me and I soon felt his shaft enter me. It was larger than I had been accustomed to, but very soft. It was a dainty morsel to the gluttonous lips through which it passed; they closed upon it with the keenest zest. Adolphe's ponderous loins settled down on mine till the hair between was matted into one mass and his shaft was caressed by every membrane in my sheath. Before he could give another thrust I was overtaken by the melting thrill. Adolphe had not yet reached his climax. He gave two or three more lazy thrusts while mine was subsiding.

"I was dreaming of Renee," he said, "when I awoke."

Exerting all my strength, I pushed him off me jealously as Lisette would have done if she had been in my place. Then I turned my back to him. He now realised what a foolish confession he had made.

"Sweet Lisette," he said, "I don't care a straw for Renee; she is not half so pretty as you are."

I obdurately shrugged my shoulders. The Lisette I impersonated would not be pacified. He snuggled up to my back and held me struggling in his arms. I could feel his stiff shaft pressed against my buttocks. He squeezed my thighs and fondled my bosoms and kissed the back of my neck, but I would not turn over. He was so excited with desire from his half-finished embrace that at last he communicated his wantonness to me I was now ready for another onset, so I turned my head and kissed him. He quickly turned me on my back and mounted fiercely to the charge. Plunge after plunge in rapid succession again woke all the sensibilities of my sheath. My mouth was buried under his moustache and the kisses kept time to the rapid play. The glow of the friction became more and more intense, spreading from the place of contact in electric waves all over my frame, and the stolen and guilty pleasure culminated in another melting thrill. Adolphe was ravished at the same time and paid me a tribute as profuse as his excitement had been long. His ample person seemed to be dissolving in my loins.

Then he sank down upon me, too weak, for some moments, to relieve me of his great weight. He soon fell sound asleep, his hand still grasping one of my bosoms and one of his heavy thighs on my own. Cautiously and by degrees I extricated myself and stole from the room, dripping at every step. Lisette was awaiting me with jealousy and impatience depicted on her countenance.

"What have you been doing all this time?" she demanded.

"The same as you have, I suppose," said I, laughing.

"I have been standing here this hour and a half," said she. "I was sobered up by the danger as soon as I got into Louis' room, and I dared not get into bed with him."

We went to our chambers, Lisette almost crying and I almost bursting with laughter. During the rest of our visit, she watched me narrowly to see that I was not a moment alone with Adolphe. She need not have been so suspicious as he was perfectly unconscious and, as for me, the curiosity of wantonness was satisfied with regard to him. When we returned to Paris, Louis rejoined the army. I had now acquired such a taste for variety that I felt much pleased at the attentions of a young duke. He sought my company on every public occasion. At last he called at my house. He had sent me a magnificent diamond necklace the day before, and it was now necessary for me to return it if I was unwilling to pursue the intrigue. In expectation of the interview I dressed myself as attentively as possible. A dress of elegant pink silk cut low in the neck displayed my bosoms to advantage and I wore the diamond necklace.

The duke saw it with a smile of pleasure the moment I entered the parlour. He came and knelt at my feet and kissed my hand, then he arose and our lips met. I consented to meet him later in the day, at a safe place of assignation, and if he had then taken his leave, all would have gone smoothly, but the duke kept kissing me and prolonged the interview. Though my husband was not expected for a day or two, still a servant was liable to enter the parlour. I rose to have him go, but he still kept his chair. With his arm around my waist, he drew me towards him and transferred his kisses from my neck to my bosoms. I bent down and kissed him on his white forehead. Desire was getting control over us both.

The duke's hand stole under my skirts and explored all the mysteries they hid. Then he lifted one of my legs over his lap and I found myself sitting astride his thighs clasped in his embrace, our lips glued together. We were insane to risk ourselves there in that position when a few hours later we could safely revel in each other's embrace. The duke produced his stiff shaft and I felt it pleading for entrance between my thighs. I half rose to tear myself from his arms, but with such feeble purpose that he pulled me down again. I sat directly upon his crest and my weight forced its entry. It filled me with a sensation of such exquisite pleasure that I abandoned myself to my uncontrollable passions.

He could not move freely, but my loins undulated to assist him, which made my ecstasy culminate. My crisis was prolonged and I had not finished melting when my husband opened the door and stood thunderstruck at the sight. I jumped backwards from the duke's arms and my skirts fell and covered my nakedness. But the duke was in the very act of spending. The sperm from his rampant crest splashed upon my dress and skirts. For a single moment I stood still and my brains whirled with incongruous thoughts, one of which was that my beautiful pink dress was spoiled by the splashes. Only a moment I stood, and then I darted from the room. I wrapped myself in a long cloak and hood as I fled through the lower hall and gained the front door.

As I passed through it, I heard the trampling of feet and the crash of furniture in the parlour above. It must have been my husband and the duke engaged in a deadly struggle. What the issue of it was, I never knew. I reached the station just as a train was about to leave. I got in it and it took me to Marseilles. Even then I did not feel safe till I had put the Mediterranean between myself and France.

Conclusion

Renee concluded. She now expected her reward. It was her turn at last.

The loins of eight of those beautiful women had been stirred to the depths by me and they had melted in my embrace. To four of them I had paid tribute in return. The night would be fittingly crowned by a tribute to the loveliest and last. She lay back at length on the cushions with Laura's back for a pillow. The charming French girl then shot a seductive glance at my face from beneath her long eyelashes and opened her graceful tapering legs.

I knelt between them and kissed the grand snow-white thighs close to the thick ruddy hair that adorned them. I planted another kiss on her smooth, round belly just over her womb. From the pink nipples of each of her plump bosoms, I sucked voluptuous kisses, and then my lips fastened on her rosebud mouth. She wound her soft white arms around me as I stretched myself on her lovely form and with her lily fingers she guided my crest to the heaven it sought. I pushed my way slowly in. It was deliciously tight and elastic and hot and juicy. I had to thrust more than once before my shaft was completely entered, which was no sooner accomplished than I felt Renee's frame shudder beneath me and then become limp and nerveless. Her arms relaxed their grasp and her sheath became loose and was flushed with moisture.

"Lie still, as you are, for a minute," she whispered, "and I shall be able to finish you."

I was in no hurry. I lay luxuriantly upon her with my crest soaking in the most inward recesses of her loins. Laura's waist still served her as a pillow and my mouth occasionally wandered from Renee's rosy mouth to kiss Laura's fat bosoms, which were so conveniently near, and my fingers searched Laura's equally convenient sheath.

Inez nestled close up to us and hid the fingers of my other hand deep between her thighs. Helene, kneeling on the other side, gently fondled my glands with her slender fingers. Zuleika, Myrzella and Virginia kissed the small of my back, shoulders and neck. My feet were abandoned to Amie and El Jelis, who sat each holding a foot between their thighs so that my toes searched their crevices. The wanton touch of nine charming and amorous women infused me rapidly with some of their own superfluous vigour. My shaft became perfectly rigid. Renee awoke to the responsibility that rested chiefly on her.

As a signal that she was again ready she darted her tongue into my mouth while I was sucking her lips. Her sheath again grew tight and I felt its inmost membranes convulsively contract and lasciviously seize my crest. I responded by giving her a deep, prolonged thrust, then I braced my toes in the hot crevices where they rested and rammed my shaft completely home again and again. Renee surged up her loins to meet each descending thrust. I felt the crisis approaching. The very marrow of my bones seemed to be distilling into my empty glands. My plunge became more rapid, until the very nerves of my shaft seemed to be laid bare to the friction. Renee redoubled her exertions. As her loins rose to meet me she gave them a rotary motion, which made her womb circle round my crest.

The supreme moment which had been coming, came at last, and I was completely ravished. My very life blood seemed to gush. I gave a deep, long groan of ecstasy and sank, an almost inanimate mass, on the panting and glowing form of Renee. She kept squeezing my shaft to complete her own rapture, and extracted a few more drops from me after I was too far gone to groan. I heard several of the ladies mingle their sighs with hers and my fingers and toes were bathed with moisture that had melted in sympathy with ours. I lay for a long time unable to stir, perfectly triumphant.

"That will make another blue-eyed boy," said Myrzella. "I feel as if I were with twins," said Renee, giving one more squeeze to my diminished shaft.

When I recovered sufficiently to be able to move, my first look was at the clock. It was near dawn, and it was necessary for me to go. The ladies helped me to dress, for I had not the strength of a kitten. Each exchanged with me a tender kiss, then I got upon the window where the rope of shawls hung—but I felt too weak to climb.

I fastened the rope around under my arms and all the ladies taking hold together lowered me safely down. I pushed my boat from the strand and set sail. The land breeze was just setting in and no sooner had I gained the offing than I descried my ship beating up and down looking for me. In an hour more I was safely on board.

A Note About the Book

Published anonymously under the pseudonym "Lord George Herbert," *A Night in a Moorish Harem* is a popular erotic novella notable for its orientalist tropes and history of legal controversy.

A Note from the Publisher

Spanning many genres, from non-fiction essays to literature classics to children's books and lyric poetry, Mint Edition books showcase the master works of our time in a modern new package. The text is freshly typeset, is clean and easy to read, and features a new note about the author in each volume. Many books also include exclusive new introductory material. Every book boasts a striking new cover, which makes it as appropriate for collecting as it is for gift giving. Mint Edition books are only printed when a reader orders them, so natural resources are not wasted. We're proud that our books are never manufactured in excess and exist only in the exact quantity they need to be read and enjoyed.

bookfinity™

Discover more of your favorite classics with Bookfinity™.

- Track your reading with custom book lists.
- Get great book recommendations for your personalized Reader Type.
- Add reviews for your favorite books.
- AND MUCH MORE!

Visit **bookfinity.com** and take the fun Reader Type quiz to get started.

Enjoy our classic and modern companion pairings!